Alice Payn

ALSO BY KATE HEARTFIELD

Armed in Her Fashion
The Course of True Love

ALICE PAYNE

ARRIVES

KATE HEARTFIELD

A TOM DOHERTY ASSOCIATES BOOK

NEW YORK

This is a work of fiction. All of the characters, organizations, and events portrayed in this novella are either products of the author's imagination or are used fictitiously.

Cover art by Cliff Nielsen
Cover design by Christine Foltzer

Edited by Lee Harris

A Tor.com Book
Published by Tom Doherty Associates
175 Fifth Avenue
New York, NY 10010

www.tor.com

Tor® is a registered trademark of
Macmillan Publishing Group, LLC.

ISBN 978-1-250-31374-4 (ebook)
ISBN 978-1-250-31373-7 (trade paperback)

First Edition: November 2018

For the women whose adventures will never be told

Alice Payne Arrives

CHAPTER ONE

Concerning a Robbery and
What Comes After

1788

THE HIGHWAYMAN KNOWN AS the Holy Ghost lurks behind the ruined church wall. Lurking has a different quality to waiting, she reflects, having time for reflection. Waiting is what she did for the first five years after Father returned from the war in America, much changed.

That's how everyone put it, that first year.—*How is Colonel Payne?—Oh, people say he is much changed.* Now, people use the same tone to say the opposite.—*How is Colonel Payne?—Oh, he's much the same.—No change? His poor daughter.*

Alice grew tired of waiting for change. Colonel Payne's poor daughter does not fade into the background; she hides in it. She's quivering in the saddle: rider, hat and gun, all cocked, after a fashion.

Ah! There it is. A carriage comes rattling around the corner, the horses' gait slowing as the slope rises toward Gibbet Hill.

Alice lurks halfway up. Behind her, on the summit, there are no trees but those of the Tyburn sort, swinging with cages and corpses, as a warning to highwaymen. It seems to have worked. She has this section of Dray Road, fenced in with trees and ruins, all to herself. The road here is a hollow way, a track worn into the ground over the centuries, its banks curving up like the bottom half of a tunnel on either side. A trap for her victims.

What a gaudy contraption the Earl of Ludderworth uses to get around the country, half-painted in gold as if he were Marie Antoinette, its four lamps lit although the sun is still bloodying the forest. Four horses, plumed. That dark bulk on the seat is the coachman and footman, both liveried like dancing monkeys, no doubt. Inside, it's big enough for four, but there will only be two. The odious earl will be travelling with his manservant. That makes four men, two of them armed with swords and probably pistols too. Loaded? Maybe, but not cocked.

Her left calf nuzzles her horse's belly. Havoc's withers twitch and he steps quietly to the right, making no sound until she taps fast with both legs and they are out in the open. By the time Havoc stops in the middle of the road, where he has stopped so many times before, she has both pistols in her hands.

"Stand and deliver!" she growls.

The first time she did this, she felt exposed, despite the hat low over her forehead, the black mask and green kerchief, the long grey cloak, the breeches and boots and gloves. She and Jane had meant it half as a lark; Jane was not convinced Alice would go through with it until she had. It was revenge, the first time, against a teacher of the pianoforte who preyed on any girl who was not sufficiently warned by her friends. Revenge, and a little much-needed money.

Now it is a regular affair, this robbery on the road. There are plenty of villains making their way through Hampshire, ready to be relieved of a purse, a blow struck in secret for womankind. Despite the fact that all the victims are men of suspect character when it comes to women, no one has made that connection, or suspected that the Holy Ghost is a woman, much less that it is Alice. All her skin is covered, lest the colour of it call to any local's mind *Colonel Payne's poor daughter.*

Today, after a dozen robberies, she does not feel exposed. She doesn't feel like Alice Payne, sitting on a horse in the middle of the road, in a disguise. She is the Holy Ghost, and she is about her vengeful business.

The coachman moves—reaching toward the seat beside him? A pistol there?

This would make a convenient moment for a partner to ride out of the woods, up to the side of the coach, a second pistol in hand. But the Holy Ghost doesn't have a partner on the road, not a human one, at least.

So she pulls the trigger in her left-hand gun and the lamp nearest her breaks and goes dark. Bullet meeting glass makes a satisfying smash that never fails to frighten cowards.

The coachman flinches, freezes.

"Hands in the air!"

His hands go high.

This is the dangerous moment. She keeps her distance, watching the windows of the coach. She's not too worried about Lord Ludderworth himself; he seems unlikely to start a fight with someone who can fight back. He presses his advances on the vulnerable: young girls, girls in service. In any event, he's a horrible shot. At more than one tedious shooting party, she's watched him fail to hit pheasants that were practically presented to him on plates. But his manservant Grigson may be another matter.

"Your money or your life! I'd rather the money, if it's all the same to you, but I'll not hesitate if it's the other."

And now, the pièce de résistance.

Six feet down the road, right beside the stopped carriage, the automaton slides out of the gorse bushes.

There are a dozen good spots for it, all along the roads of this county. Three of them happen to be near churches, and one near an abbey, which has given rise to the Holy Ghost nickname. A reputation is good for a highwayman. When people know what to expect, they aren't so afraid as to do foolish things. A well-known robber who puts on a predictable show is an institution, and the good people of England will hand over their tolls with due resignation and respect.

In the twilight, the sight of Alice's automaton sends shivers down her own skin. The carved wooden head, painted white with blue eyes and red lips, as still as a Madonna's. The grey cloak, the same colour as her own, the hood brought over the head. The outstretched hand.

The coachman crosses himself.

The coach window clicks open a crack, wide enough to admit a gun—she breathes, keeps her seat still and remains calm—but instead, out sneaks a purse in pudgy, ringed fingers—the hand of Lord Ludderworth himself. The hand that lifted her skirt when she was fourteen, that has squeezed every housemaid's breast between London and Bristol.

The little purse lands in the wooden hand and the automaton stands motionless for a moment, then flips its hand to let the purse drop into the box. The box clacks on the cart rails, a few yards up the hill along the side of the road to where Alice sits on Havoc.

The automaton lets Alice keep her distance, and it gives the villains a show for their money. A story to tell.

It is noisy, but it is not meant to fool anyone. Everyone knows it is a machine and that only inspires all the more awe. Ghosts and fairies litter history, but machines that can move like humans are the stuff of dreams.

Jane's work never ceases to amaze her. Her darling Jane, working on her gears and springs in her study, believing that one day, her toys and curiosities will bring Utopia. For now, this one brings Alice a living and brings a little justice to the world, and that is good enough for Alice.

Alice never lets the pistol in her right hand droop, keeps her wide gaze on the coachman, the footman, the open window. At the edge of her vision, she pokes the hook she's attached to the end of her riding crop into the handle of the box, lifts it by the handle, drops it into her lap. She unties the purse, still watching the coach, lifts a coin to her mouth and bites.

The automaton nods its head, as it always does after three minutes.

There is a long silence.

She shifts in the saddle. Almost done. Almost safe.

Havoc's head snaps up, but he's a steady horse, steadier than his mistress. He stands and waits.

"That'll do," she says, trying not to let the relief into her voice. "Ride on. The toll's paid."

An easy night's work. The manservant Grigson never made his appearance. She watches the coach rattle up Gibbet Hill for a moment.

Then she ties the purse to her belt. She jumps Havoc up onto the bank and rides him more or less the same way. She'll have to ride fast if she's to beat the frightened coachman to Fleance Hall with enough time to change her clothes and fix her hair.

And then, after the world is asleep, she'll return for the automaton. It has slid back into its hiding spot in the bushes.

She grins as she rides through the paths that she and Havoc know well. The new purse bangs against her hip. That will buy Father a month's freedom from his creditors, at least.

At the sound of hoofbeats, she snaps her head around, as beneath her Havoc's muscles run taut as rope.

Behind her, and not very far, a man on a grey horse. He's hatless, and she recognizes his face at once. Grigson.

The manservant was never in the coach. He was riding behind, waiting before the bend in the road, waiting to pursue the thief rumoured to haunt Dray Road.

Damn Lord Ludderworth. So stingy he'd rather risk his right-hand man than lose a bit of gold.

The bank is easily five feet higher than the road here and she can see the carriage rattling along up the hill, bearing the earl to safety while his servant tries to capture the most notorious highwayman this side of London. Well, he won't get his chance. Havoc is a fast horse and she knows these woods like no one else does. There's a deer path up ahead that will take her to a winding, deep creek ford where she can double back without being seen, if she times it well.

As she steers Havoc's nose that way, she glances behind her.

Damn! Two more men, on her right; Grigson approaching behind.

The one way they won't expect her to veer is left.

She pulls Havoc to the left and spurs him to a gallop. The carriage is rattling up the hill, and here on the higher ground the banks flatten out, so that the road is no longer a hollow way. Havoc does not even break his stride as his hoofs hit the dirt of the road, just behind the carriage. She'll cross behind it and—

A horse whinnies in fear, up in the team, and the carriage careens off the road, rocks as the wheels hit the grassy banks.

Alice keeps Havoc at full speed. Her leg grazes an old milestone stuck in the grassy bank. She turns parallel to the road again, heading up the hill, to put the carriage between herself and the three pursuers. Typical of Lord Ludderworth, to wait until he was out of danger before loosing his ambush!

There are few trees here to hide her. She glances back: the three horsemen were surprised by her sudden turn back to the road and she's put a little distance between them. Once she crests the hill, and is out of their sight for a moment, she'll double back to the right and find the creek bed.

She glances once more at the road and squints, frowning. The carriage is out of sight; it must have been travelling faster than she realized and crested the hill already, despite going off track for a moment. That must be a fine coachman to get the horses in hand so quickly after they took fright at Havoc's approach. Perhaps they bolted.

The air seems to shimmer beside the road like a soap bubble, just there by the old milestone. It's mere fancy—everything looks strange at twilight—and she can't afford a second look.

Over the hill, hidden from view for a moment, Havoc veers back over the road toward the creek. She races along the most winding paths to Fleance Hall, where Alice Payne is expected.

CHAPTER TWO

In Which the Wrong Mistress
Is Persuaded

1889

PRUDENCE OPENS THE HACKNEY door before it stops and jumps onto the snow. Her motherfucking Victorian boot heels stick with every step, but after she gets out of the drift and up onto the frozen ground, she can run, holding her skirts.

The Mayerling hunting lodge sprawls red-roofed against the bare Austrian hills. It's just past dawn, with a murmur of cowbells and lowing not too distant. Here, though, everything is quiet.

She had better be wrong. Oh, she had better be wrong. Mary Vetsera is only seventeen, and Crown Prince Rudolf has only been screwing her for a few months. Besides, Mary's a baroness, hardly the one he'd choose for a suicide pact. He's always used Mitzi for playing to his Byronic self-image: his Viennese demimonde "dancer," so nicely shocking to the Austrian court.

It has taken Prudence seventy-one attempts at 1889 to convince Mitzi to refuse to die with Rudolf, to report his suggestion of suicide to the police.

Seventy failures and now, at last, success. Two nights ago, Rudolf came to Mitzi and she refused to die with him. They cried. Prudence was there, the maid in the next room, listening, ready to comfort Mitzi the moment her lover left. Rudolf even promised to get off the morphine. If he doesn't kill himself, he'll live with his syphilis for decades. Everything will be fine.

Mitzi has told the police twice that Rudolf is suicidal. They never do a damn thing about it. But at last, Prudence thought she had saved them from their suicide pact. Mitzi was upset, but resolute. Strong. Any moment now, she should hear from General Almo, saying: *You've done it. Mission complete. Come home.*

Home being the year 2145, for lack of anything better.

And then yesterday afternoon, the letter arrived, from Rudolf, saying goodbye. It might seem a lover's farewell, nothing more—but Prudence has misgivings. No word from Almo, no word from the future that the past has been changed. She asked her most useful gossip where Rudolf had gone that day, and she heard: *Mayerling. With Mary Vetsera.*

She runs to the gatehouse and peers inside. One guard, but not at his post: he's in the courtyard with another man, hitching two horses to a calèche. It's six thirty in the morning, early for Rudolf to have asked for a carriage, but then this is a hunting lodge.

She can tell the other man by his whiskers: Loschek. Rudolf's valet. The man who always sleeps in the room next to Rudolf and whatever woman Rudolf has in his bed on any given night.

Rudolf has sent the man in the bedroom next to his own outside, away from him. To hitch the horses? Or to get him away?

She darts inside the gate and around the corner to the window Mitzi snuck out of a few months before, to get away from Rudolf in one of his moods. As Mitzi's maid, Prudence knows well enough which room Rudolf uses as his bedroom when he has a lover here.

He had better be sleeping. Oh, she had better be wrong.

Goddamn those Misguideds. The damage they cause! The more they encourage Rudolf's liberal tendencies, with their agent-tutors and agent-friends, the angrier Rudolf becomes with his tyrannical father. The worse Rudolf's melancholy, the more entrenched Rudolf's conviction that there is no point to his own life beyond sex and drink. The man who could save the world from the First World War, squandered to syphilis and depression.

The Misguideds are now trying to fix the suicide problem, just as Prudence is, but they're working with Rudolf. The Farmers can't get close to him, so Prudence was assigned to Mitzi. Ten years ago. For ten years she's been reliving 1889, getting it wrong, getting it wrong.

She puts her boot on the drainpipe and thrusts her knife between the window and the sill. No matter where she goes in human history, she always carries a knife.

The window budges, at last, and she pulls it open and heaves herself through.

This time, there's no chair in the hallway on the other side, so she falls to her stomach, knocking the wind out of herself. She waits, prepares herself to pose as yet another new mistress if anyone but Rudolf comes, but there's no one. Silence.

A shadow moves, far down at the other end of the hall. A guard.

She'd like to unbutton the awful boots but there's no time so she tiptoes as softly as she can, opens one door and then another.

She knows, as soon she opens the right room, that she was not wrong. She's seen Rudolf's dead face many times. The image of her failure.

She steps inside and closes and locks the door behind

her. She can't be discovered here. There might still be time; he might be alive.

He's slumped on the floor, blood trickling from his mouth.

Gore on the wall behind him.

There's an empty glass; there's a gun; there's Mary, on the bed, not sleeping.

Prudence kneels by his side, this asshole of a prince whom she's never met but whose life she has been trying to save for ten years. Another failure. Under her fingertips, no pulse.

"Major Zuniga."

She stands quickly and turns, dizzy for a moment. On a chair: a red felt hat, with black feathers.

General Almo stands in his fatigues, a time portal behind him. Why the hell did he shimmer here himself? He's never done that, not in any of her past failures.

Any moment now, the valet will return. Almo turns and locks the door, as if he's had the same thought. The key was in the keyhole. There is a hairbrush on the dresser, and by the bed a pair of dove-coloured women's shoes ...

"It's earlier this time," she says, and her voice is full as if she wants to weep, although she has no more reason to weep than she's had the last seventy times. But this time, she thought she had it. She saved Mitzi's life. She thought she'd saved Rudolf's too.

"And he's chosen a different partner, I see."

She nods. "Mary Vetsera. She's just a girl. But now we know that's a possibility. It won't happen again, sir."

"There won't be an again. I'm reassigning you."

She has to lean against something but there's nothing to lean on, nothing that isn't covered with Rudolf's blood. She steps closer to the general, rooting herself in the movement.

"Sir, I can do this."

"No. You can't."

He's a big man, and seems even bigger here, in this room. There is too much history here for these four walls to contain.

"If it's . . . I know there are limits to what a woman of colour can do in this setting, but I can work with Vetsera just as I worked with Mitzi. I've got a prep package to be an American artist, like Edmonia Lewis. Vetsera could be convinced to take art lessons."

"It's not that. We're shutting down this mission. Putting our resources elsewhere, in 2016. Let's try 2016 again."

"But 2016 is *completely fucked*," she says, trying to keep her voice even. "You know that. Sir. We have to go back earlier."

He shakes his head. "Obsession happens to all of us but we have to see it for what it is. It's my fault. I wanted this too. I let you stay here far too long. But no single moment of history is everything. It's a long war, Major Zuniga. If we fight one battle forever, it will never end."

She nods, because she doesn't trust herself to speak. He's right. The war of attrition for human history will never end, not if the Farmers keep fighting the Misguideds battle to battle, moment to moment.

General Almo is right. It is pointless to keep trying to push history one way while the Misguideds are trying to push it in another. But he doesn't have the courage to do what needs to be done. The only way to end this war, to end all wars, is to stop anyone from changing history ever again.

CHAPTER THREE

Companions; or, How Alice
Is Transformed

1788

ALICE LOSES HER PURSUERS at the creek bed. Havoc picks his way back up the bank and into the woods, where he knows the paths to home.

She urges Havoc to go faster, although it's nearly too dark to see. She does not dare light the mica lantern in her saddlebag. She needs to return unseen. By now, Lord Ludderworth's carriage will have arrived at Fleance Hall. Alice is meant to be at the door with Father to greet their guest, to distract his attention from the fewness of servants with bluster and goodwill.

There's a lantern at the second servants' entrance, around the back of the house, where Jane waits, holding a candlestick.

She takes Havoc by the bridle and says, "I'll tie him here

and stable him later before the groom does his rounds."

The fact that the groom is also kept busy being the coachman, the footman and man-of-all-work makes taking horses out of the stable very convenient. Before Father went away to war, Fleance Hall had nine servants. Now it has four: a cook, a housemaid, the groom and the indefinable Satterthwaite, her father's butler/valet/man-of-business.

"Your gown is just inside." Jane points. "What kept you, Alice? Your father has been asking—he thinks I've gone up to your room to help you with some womanly requirement."

"Time for that later," Alice says, and kisses her, snaking one arm around her waist.

"Go on," Jane hisses, pushing Alice, but she's smiling. "Your father's guest will be here any moment."

Alice slips through the propped-open door into the little anteroom, where her clothes are laid out on the bench. Her best yellow gown, of course. Jane's lit two candles on the wall sconces, but it's still gloomy. She kicks off the high riding boots and wriggles out of the breeches. She's shivering in her shift when Jane slides in and closes the door behind her.

Ten years they've lived together now at Fleance Hall. It was Father's idea to bring his cousin's ward here to be Alice's companion, when he went away to America to fight. Alice was only twenty-two then, and Father held great hopes that she'd marry. Truth be told, she's never done much to encourage proposals, and actively discouraged them whenever any of her lovers got too close. In those early years, while Father was away, Jane was a friend. Over the last year, she's given Alice a reason to discourage proposals forevermore.

She plops the purse full of coins and rings into Jane's white hand.

"Ah, you and Laverna got your man."

"We did." Laverna is the name that Jane gave the automaton, early on: the patron goddess of thieves.

Alice wriggles into her slim modesty petticoat, then pushes the clothes over enough on the bench to give herself room to sit, and points her toe. Each white stocking rolls up under Jane's white fingertips, which brush the tops of Alice's bare knees, under the modesty petticoat.

"You know," Jane says, "I was never jealous of any of your lovers, but sometimes I feel a little jealous of Laverna."

"She is your creation, darling."

"All the more reason. I don't trust anything I build. Do you remember the walking doll I made for Freddy Combles last Christmas? I swear it used to migrate through the house in the night. I was glad to be rid of it."

She glances up and Alice offers a weary smile.

"What is it, Alice? What did keep you, on the road?"

"Ludderworth's servants chased me. Don't worry, Jane, they didn't get close. But they did delay me. I can't believe Lord Ludderworth isn't here already. He must have stopped to wait for his servants. Lucky for me he did."

Alice puts her hand on the petticoat, keeping Jane's hand there, and Jane slides her fingers up the inside of her thigh. Under the shift, under the petticoat, there is nothing between them. Jane's thumb and finger find their places with absolute confidence as Jane leans into her and says against Alice's lips: "Later."

Alice groans theatrically and stands up so Jane can wrap the stays around her body and lace them down the front, over the stomacher, shaping Alice into the role of Miss Payne. Jane knows every inch of her body, where it will give and where it will swell. Jane slides the wooden busk between shift and stays, and together they tie the yellow petticoat around her waist. A gauze fichu over the shoulders, then she slips into the gown like a jacket and Jane closes it in front, working fast, thrusting the pins into the stays.

"Damn it," Jane swears around the pin in her mouth. "It's crooked here."

"Never mind that," Alice says. She steps into the yellow silk shoes and picks up the white-ribboned cap, the only thing left on the bench, and pins it quickly over the back of her hair. It was braided under the hat, and the frizzes that have come free around her forehead will look just fine with the cap.

It's only Lord Ludderworth, anyway. If her gown is pinned crookedly and her hair a little wild, what does it matter? It's been years since she could afford to keep a lady's maid. She is thirty-two years old, keeping herself and her family under this roof by dint of adventure, and she does not give a damn if her bodice is straight.

She tugs the sides of the fichu a little more closely together over her cleavage, and runs down the hallway, leaving Jane to gather the cast-off highwayman's clothes and hide them in her study. The housemaid never ventures in there; she's afraid of all the machines and instruments, and especially of the frogs in jars.

Alice runs, one hand holding her skirt, the other skimming the walls that she loves, although the paper is peeling. Through the parlour, empty, lit only by embers. Voices in the hall just inside the main door. She runs past Satterthwaite at the door and comes skidding to a halt on the chequerboard floor, the only part of the big house that is scrubbed to a polish and brightly lit.

The four men in the room turn to look at her.

Father says, "Alice! At last!"

Standing beside Father is not Lord Ludderworth, or

even Lord Ludderworth's coachman or footman, but the manservant who chased her on his horse. He's wet with sweat and too alarmed to do anything but bow his head.

"You remember John Grigson. Lord Ludderworth's manservant. These two men with him are servants of the earl's household as well."

"Of course," Alice says, bowing her head. "Mr. Grigson."

"Miss Payne," says Grigson, glancing from Alice to her father and back. She's seen people do this her whole life, contrasting her father's pale skin with her own. She takes after her Caribbean mother, whom she does not remember. Grigson is black himself, though, and usually it is white people who have more difficulty with the existence of Alice. It dawns that his hesitation, his glancing from face to face, has little to do with her. He's had a shock. God, could he have some idea that she is the highwayman?

"Lord Ludderworth went on ahead of us," he says. "How can it be that he has not arrived?"

"What do you mean?" Father barks. "You mean to say that your master is somewhere out there on the road, still?"

Grigson shakes his head. "That he is not, Colonel. I'd stake my life."

"Then where, man?"

CHAPTER FOUR

On the Nuclear Option, with Cocktails

2070

PRUDENCE PAUSES OUTSIDE the yellow-brick house and pulls out her EEG scanner. Just to be safe. Two people inside, both of them neutrals. She chose Helmut and Rati with care: radical conservatives, young enough with nothing to lose and smart enough to have dangerous confidence in their own decisions. To the scanner, that's neither Farmer nor Misguided, but neutral. A person with extreme tendencies on either end of a spectrum sometimes registers the same as a moderate.

The retina lock on the door is disguised as an old-fashioned peephole, because the only houses that would have such security in this part of suburban Toronto would be drug houses. Prudence would rather not attract any official attention. No records.

The lock clicks and she turns the doorknob.

"I'm home," she says, stepping into the dim hall.

She means it as a joke, but it feels true. Even before she set up her rogue project in this ugly little house, Prudence Zuniga always had a place to stay in 2070. Most of her friends—well, colleagues—are here, and this time around, her sister.

This year is the destination of choice for discerning time travellers.

2070: Later than the biggest waves of History War refugees and the backlash to them.

2070: Twenty-one years earlier than the beginning of the History War itself, although the first rumblings of that war are now only a year away. Teleosophy begins as an intelligence wing of the U.S. military in 2071. Twenty years later, it will explode into a global war between the Farmers and the so-called Guides.

The technology of 2070 is advanced enough to make life comfortable. Time travel is new but available for those who can pay; upstream in earlier centuries, the only travellers are military like Prudence. The war won't get bad enough to visibly affect contemporary life until after the Anarchy hits in 2139. That leaves plenty of time for a human to live out a life. Sure, the climate's a mess already by 2070, but it's a catastrophe, not yet an apocalypse.

Visit 2070: It's Not an Apocalypse. Yet. This Time.

She hasn't written marketing copy in... what? How

many years of her life? Too many to do the math. The voice of it in her head twists itself ever more cynically but never goes silent. Of course, propaganda isn't all that different. She spent several years behind a desk doing propaganda for the Mao and Peron projects, and various European Union campaigns, before Almo recruited her out of the communications branch.

Farmer agents never lie unless it's absolutely necessary. She's learned how to make the truth do what she wants it to do.

If Project Shipwreck works, though, there will be a lot less demand for her unique set of skills.

Helmut and Rati emerge at the top of the basement stairs.

"Anything I should know about?" she asks.

Helmut shakes his head. "We're still running reliability checks. Getting better. Point-two percent."

Prudence sighs. Not nearly good enough. But she won't wait any longer.

"You look exhausted," Rati says. "Is 1889 not going well?"

They are both looking at her with concern. They're too goddamn young, too new, to know that it's perfectly normal to be exhausted.

"Not going at all, anymore. General Almo's closed it down."

"Closed it down?" Rati asks. She's the sharper of the two. "You mean he . . . gave up?"

Prudence walks the room, checks their work. They've been busy. They're dedicated, these two. They're ready. "He wanted to reassign me to goddamn 2016, which if you ask me is too late to do any good for the timeline, and too early to do any good for the History War. I convinced him to send me here to do Berlin Convention sabotage instead."

If he suspects anything, he'll suspect that Prudence wants to spend time with her sister. It's one more reason she chose to make this time and place the headquarters for Project Shipwreck. She has a plausible reason to want to come here.

"The leaders won't lead," she sloganeers. "So we have to."

Rati frowns. "Now? But you said . . ."

When they began, three years ago in Prudence's life-line, it was an experiment to see how much EEG-scanner coverage they could achieve, worldwide. They were going to turn the network over to Teleosophic Core Command, or said they were.

Prudence, Rati and Helmut have mainly kept up that fiction even among themselves, but the network has been basically complete for months and they haven't discussed handing it over to the TCC. Even if they could convince the TCC to send a generation of Misguideds downstream, they could never convince the TCC to end time travel altogether. Project Shipwreck won't be nearly as effective if they allow the enemy to develop counterstrike ability. Mutually assured destruction is exactly what Prudence and her protégés are trying to avert.

So the three of them have drifted, from rogues to traitors.

"Almo doesn't have the stomach to win," says Helmut. "He just gave up on preventing the First World War."

"Exactly," says Prudence. "The Command has just shown it is not interested in putting an end to this war. Too many generals behind desks and not enough of them out in the field to see what the enemy is doing. I've seen, over the last ten years, just how fanatical the Misguideds can be. There is no winning against a cult in a war of attrition. The only way is to burn it all down. Almo can't see that. So it's up to us."

They're quiet.

"And what about the 1788 component?" Rati asks.

"I've chosen the naïf and I'll go today. Jane Hodgson. You two know that name?"

Helmut shakes his head, but Rati says, "The inventor of the helidrone?"

Prudence smiles. "Just the kind of person we want, don't you think? She dies in poverty, so I think the reward, and the lure of a scientific machine she's never seen, will do the trick."

Helmut shakes his head. "It's a weak spot, but I don't know what to do about it. I'd go myself, happily, but we just can't be sure that the causality won't glitch. I was hoping to figure it out, but—"

Prudence raises her hand. "Hodgson will work out. And if she doesn't, there are plenty of other people in 1788 who will take the job."

Helmut nods. "All right. Once that's in place, we're ready."

"Ready? You just said point-two percent!"

He blushes. "Point-two percent may be as low as I'll ever be able to get it. EEG scanning has inherent limits, and there will always be some false positives."

"OK. Let's think about the consequences of that. The global population of Misguideds, as of July 1, 2070, will be roughly two-point-two-six billion. Right? Which gives us a false positive of . . . let's see . . . oh, four and a half million people. Four and a half million people who are actually neutrals, or maybe even Farmers. People like us."

Helmut frowns, and his face goes pink.

"Yes," says Rati, glancing at him, and back at Prudence. "But it's not as if we're killing them."

"No, we're not killing them," she says. Her voice still

sounds like a rusty hinge. "Probably. But it's the god-damn nuclear option, isn't it?"

Their eyes go wide. Shit. She has to tread more carefully here. She's taking them for granted.

These two kids are working with second-rate equipment, putting all of Rati's ill-gotten funds toward the power cells. They've disguised their workshop to fit the period, as much as possible, and to fit their cover story, should any of their fellow Farmers find them. These two young people have chosen not only to blow up their own chances at making a better world, but to blow up everyone else's chances too. She's already asking too much of them, but goddammit, she's going to ask for a little fucking humanity too.

"Look," she says. "Our energy supply is going to be extremely touch-and-go as it is. Nobody has ever done anything like this before. Ever. We're moving two billion people five centuries downstream. I would like to have a little wiggle room in my calculations. OK?"

Helmut nods, although he's still a faint salmon colour. White people: always showing their emotions in their skin. Date the Walking Biogenuine Mood Avatar. Never Be in Doubt of How He Feels Again.

They both nod, dutifully, devotedly. They are exhausted, poor tadpoles. And she needs to do a better job of morale.

"Let's get a drink," she says. "I think Orbital Decays are still popular in Toronto in 2070. You like cocktails, Helmut? Of course you do. Everybody likes cocktails."

They close down the displays, power down the cooling fans and the Faraday decoy rig.

She hangs back, trudging behind them like a chaperone while Helmut and Rati chatter their way down the sidewalk, into the streets of Toronto. It takes twenty minutes to get to the gentrified part of the neighbourhood. They order their cocktails and sit in a dark booth in the back, watching the life of an ordinary bar. Rati has her scanner on the table. It blinks orange, green, blue, as people pass by their table.

"You're worried," Prudence says, grimacing a bit at the sourness of her Orbital Decay. The mix of shrub syrup and gin always takes a few sips to taste anything but awful.

"Not worried," Rati says, stirring her own Decay so the tapioca pearls dance and swirl in the martini glass. "Just . . . wondering. Thinking about the timing. You keep a diary, right? You've been at this longer than I have. Can you really know that this is the best of all plausible worlds?"

"I'm sure it isn't," Prudence says. "But I know it isn't the worst."

CHAPTER FIVE

In Which Mr. Grigson Gives His Account

1788

"**BUT DO YOU MEAN TO SAY,**" says Father, "that you and His Lordship did not travel together, or that you did? Elucidate."

Father is florid already, well past the heady certainty that no one can tell he's had two mugs of cider if he pronounces his diphthongs with austerity, and venturing into gleeful indifference.

Grigson glances at her again. "I do not wish to frighten Miss Payne, but—"

"Miss Payne does not frighten easily," says Father, loudly, regretfully.

It is irritating, the way Father becomes all the more imperious after each of his absent episodes. Mr. Brown the groom found him wandering on the hills again, just last week, and Alice held Father's hand while he stared into the posset of cream and strong sack that Cook made for him, while all the servants tried not to show their concern. And then the next morning, he was back to being this other new version of himself, disagreeable and unkind, as if in compensation for his vulnerability the night before.

Grigson looks back at her. She smiles sweetly.

"We were expecting trouble," Grigson says. "There have been so many tales of the Holy Ghost in this county lately. So my lord asked me to ride a little behind, so that if he were robbed, I could give chase. It all happened just as he thought it would. Just as the stories say: the man appeared, and then the apparition. A creature of wood and gears, if you ask me, although I could only see the shape of it from where I was. As soon as the coachman had driven my lord up Gibbet Hill, I spurred my horse and my companions did the same. The man veered back across the road, around the carriage and out of view over the hill. The carriage horses spooked and ran up onto the road bank, but we three followed the highwayman. I lost him in a creek bed. I had half a mind then to return and find the automaton and smash it to bits—"

Alice's intake of breath is loud; the man pauses; she covers it up by fluttering her hand to her mouth, hoping she looks overwhelmed at his manly energy. He *is* handsome. Good arms, nice legs.

She has always dismantled Laverna during the night, after her prey has passed. If they find it, there is no clue that could betray her, and she does not *think* anyone would trace it back to Jane—people tend to leave her to putter about in her study, the harmless companion, bookish, fancies herself a scholar... Still. Laverna is theirs, their private secret, and she does not want their secrets smashed or studied.

"Go on, man," says Father, "and never mind what you had half a mind to do. Where was His Lordship then?"

"Upon the road, or so I thought. A fear struck me that perhaps we had driven the highwayman to take some desperate action. Perhaps he thought we'd recognized him. So we returned to the road, back to the spot where we left it, and then rode as hard as our horses would go, straight to Fleance Hall."

He pauses, and takes a deep, shuddering breath.

"I did not pass the carriage. And it was not here when I arrived."

"What do you mean?" Alice asks sharply. "It could not have vanished. There are no side roads, no paths big enough to take a carriage, not between here and Gibbet Hill."

That's the very reason she chose that spot to waylay Lord Ludderworth, once she heard that Father had invited him to Fleance Hall. He was a fish in a pond. So where is he now?

"You mean to say the whole carriage has vanished?" Father asks.

"And the three men in it."

"Three? What three? Who was with the earl? Your tale is all tangled."

"I mean, Colonel, that the earl was driven by his coachman, and that there was a footman too, riding on the seat."

"It must be just on the hill somewhere," says Alice. "Perhaps the coachman couldn't get the horses back onto the road, and decided to wait for help."

"Begging your pardon," says Grigson, "but there are few trees on the hill. Not much to hide a carriage behind."

"You could have passed very near to it without seeing, in the dark," she says. "Or they turned around to drive back to London, although why they would, when they were three miles from Fleance Hall, I can't imagine."

It must have been fancy, that shimmer in the air beside the road near the last place she saw the carriage. But perhaps her fancy had some cause. Perhaps her eye caught sight of something her mind did not have time to understand.

"Satterthwaite," says Father, his brows knit. "Have the groom ride to the New House and fetch Captain Auden."

Is he getting up a search party? They'll find the automaton. She has to get out before them and dismantle it. Damn that earl! Where can he have gone?

"What do you want with Wray Auden, father?" Alice asks. "Do you think the carriage passed our lane in the night and went on to New House? It's possible, I suppose, although we have the lantern lit."

"That is possible, yes," says Father, adopting a pompous set to his jowls to camouflage his suppressing of a belch, "but I want Captain Auden because he's the parish constable. There's been at least one crime done tonight, and maybe more than one. It's time this highwayman was caught."

CHAPTER SIX

By Which It Will Appear
That Grace Is Uneasy

2070

PRUDENCE'S SISTER GRACE LIVES in Capsule, the tent city north of Toronto, about an hour by solarbus from the yellow-brick suburban town house where Prudence's rogue cell has set up operations. On this visit, Prudence won't be staying on the air mattress on the floor of Grace's tent, curtained off from where Grace sleeps with Alexei every night.

Tonight, though, Grace is alone, cooking plantains on the burner. In the low light from the electric lantern, this woman, in this tent, could be anywhere and anytime. But this is Canada in 2070, when it's warm enough to grow good plantains north of Toronto, yet not hot enough for drought-pricing to drive up the cost of bread.

Prudence and Grace have lived in Capsule since they

arrived in 2040 as children, with the other refugees from 2140. It took five years for their parents to save up enough to send them upstream by a century, to send them away.

That migration was the first mass shimmer, controlled not by a single travelling teleosopher but by a commercial operator. That company was the first to figure out how to lock on to the EEG signatures and shimmer people en masse.

"You're back," Grace says, glancing up. "You see them this time?"

Grace has never shimmered since they arrived; it's far too expensive for civilians. For Prudence, it's part of the job. Her shimmer belt, military issue, will take her anywhere in human history.

She's seen their parents many times, in many different circumstances, before their deaths in the riots in 2140, mere months after they sent their children away. On leave between attempts at the Rudolf Project, she used to visit Dale Zuniga and Mary Rho as young, childless adults, without their knowing who she was. But not these last few months. She doesn't want to sour anything in their family timeline. The slightest decision could be the border between a world with Grace in it and a world without her.

She shakes her head. "Business only, this last trip."

"Of course." There's an edge to Grace's voice tonight. Prudence knows that voice better than she knows anything in this world. She knows exactly how long it will take before whatever is bothering Grace comes like a torrent out of her, before Grace's eyes flash and the shadows under her brows darken and then, how long it will be after that before Grace laughs at herself and the skies clear.

It seems impossible that Prudence could know her sister to the very pore and that Grace has only existed for the past five months of Prudence's life. And yet, both those facts are true. Her diary says so. Grace only came into existence after a Misguided team went to 1932. The Farmer intelligence is spotty on what exactly those Misguideds did. Whatever it was, how could it possibly have affected the coitus between Mary Rho and Dale Zuniga in 2130?

And yet.

Here is Grace.

A sister Prudence now remembers knowing for her entire life. She does not remember a life without her. Only her diary does. History—her history—changed. And for once, this is a change she does not abhor.

Grace hands her a camp-plate with a flour tortilla, some dark red beans and three golden slices of plantain. This was how their dad used to cook, even after they moved to Canada. When they got the news that the mass refugee migration would go to 2040, he tried to cheer them up by joking that at least it wouldn't be so cold that you couldn't get good mangoes.

The sisters sit cross-legged on cushions.

Prudence eats, folding the tortilla around the warm, rich beans.

"It's good."

"Sure it's good."

"Where's Alexei?"

"Working. He has a lead on something."

Prudence nods. She doesn't ask too many questions about how Grace and Alexei get by. She pays for what she eats, when she visits, and a little extra when Grace lets her get away with it.

"How go the wars, Major Zuniga?" Grace asks, looking at Prudence as if there's some clue in her braids, her T-shirt, her khakis.

Farmers never wear a uniform in the field; the whole idea is that they're supposed to blend in to whatever period they're infiltrating. She travels with whatever shimmering equipment the Command deems necessary, and with a holstered EEG scanner under her clothing. EEG remote scanners won't be invented until 2135, so very few civilians have them in earlier time periods, but all Farmers carry them. They use them in the field to identify likely marks for propaganda, or particularly dangerous Misguideds. The little black device at her hip is no different in kind from the global EEG surveillance system that Helmut and Rati have been working on for five years.

How to answer Grace's question? How to tell her that she has failed, horribly, that the last ten years of her life are worse than a waste? That she is responsible for the deaths of millions? That she can't be a part of it, even a witness to it anymore?

"If I told you, I'd have to kill your grandma," Prudence says lightly. It's an old shimmer joke, and it's not funny.

Grace smiles anyway, at something she's thinking. "You remember how Uncle Mads used to tell us that piss-poor joke about the pterodactyl?"

"Ugh," says Prudence, nodding, laughter filling her chest. "What was it? 'Because the *p* is silent'? Shit. I can't believe he tried it every single time. Like we're going to forget from the last time."

"Maybe he was an undercover teleo," gasps Grace, wiping her eye. "He was caught in a loop."

"It would explain a lot."

They let the laughter trickle to nothing, the tent warm with the sweet smell of plantain and their silence. Grace's mouth squirms, as if with the remnants of laughter, but there's something more to it.

Prudence is sick of waiting, out of the habit of letting

time unfurl on its own, and the relief of laughing with her sister makes her eager for more of her, more of this closeness.

"Weh de go ahn, gial?" Prudence says it softly, putting her head to one side. They don't speak Belizean Creole often, now, but it was once the language of secrets and the promise of secrets between them. Their father's language.

Grace drops her gaze, shakes her head. "Prudence. You're going to look at me."

"Oh, yes, I'm a horrible person. With eyes. You want me to avert my gaze? What?"

"No, damn, I mean you're going to *look* at me. Like you do. Like you know a secret you can't tell me."

"Well, maybe I do. It's the job, Grace."

"No, it's not. That's not what I'm talking about. It's—well, Alexei and I have been talking about trying. For a baby."

CHAPTER SEVEN

Alice Investigates, with Results That Will Hereinafter Appear

1788

AS SOON AS THE searchers ride out across the brush-covered pasture between Fleance Hall and Gibbet Hill, Alice and Jane saddle Havoc and Thunder and ride down the road to dismantle the automaton. They wear cloaks over their gowns, and daggers tucked down behind their busks, but for once they have no need of disguise or sub-terfuge. If they're found, they'll say they were trying to help the searchers.

They can hear the shouts of the men, and see their lanterns among the trees, but they don't meet anyone. Jane gets to work dismantling Laverna while Alice keeps watch, wheeling Havoc back and forth on the road.

It was Father who taught her to ride, in better days.

At last, Jane is done with her work. Laverna, the little box and the rails all just barely fit in their four saddlebags, when dismantled.

After Laverna has been safely hidden in Jane's study, the lovers make hot chocolate in the empty kitchen and take the tray out to the drawing room. It feels as though they have the house to themselves, and they nearly do. Past midnight, Cook and the housemaid are in bed, and Satterthwaite, the groom and Father are out with the search party. Everything is quiet.

In one corner of the drawing room, two chaises meet at right angles. They each take one of them and stretch out under blankets to wait for news. Their heads loll, close, and Alice wrenches her neck around to kiss Jane's temple, under her blond curls.

"They could return any time," Jane whispers. "Careful."

Alice sighs, and turns away. "I am sick of hiding. We should get a cottage somewhere. Just the two of us."

"But you love Fleance Hall."

"Well, I wouldn't give up Fleance Hall. I'd just keep you as a paramour, all hidden behind walls of brambles. Don't worry. I'd give you your machines to keep you company."

"Hmph."

She says nothing more, and at last Alice turns to see if she has hurt her, but Jane's eyes are closed.

Alice slips off her chaise, kneels by Jane and watches her sleeping face for a few breaths. She goes to the writing table, scratches a few lines on a piece of paper and tucks it into Jane's blanket. Alice doesn't want to sleep. She wants to know what she saw on the road.

Havoc is grumpy at this third ride of the night, and he refuses to graze when she ties him near the old milestone where the carriage went off the road. He snorts and shuffles his feet, watching her peer at the ground.

The sun is nearly up and she can see things in the cool morning twilight that she did not see in the night: hoof marks and wheel prints. They don't make any sense. The marks of the carriage go straight off the road, up the muddy bank, and then they simply stop. No change of distance between the hooves. No sign that the horses paused or turned back to the road.

Lord Ludderworth is the very last person on earth she would have imagined running away with the fairies.

So what is it, then? That aura she saw. It may have been her imagination, but perhaps imagination saw what her reason could not. Perhaps there was something that caught her eye about this place—but what?

A gleam catches her eye on the ground, a few steps away in a patch of daisies.

She kneels on the ground and parts the flowers. A glint of wire, and a gleam like brass.

It's a mechanism. A device of some kind, with nine wheels overlaid on each other, round and gleaming like the gears of a clock, about as big as her hand. Something of Jane's?

"Looking for something?"

She falls back onto her arse, her skirt in the mud, and thrusts the mechanism into her pocket.

Wray Auden's several paces away, down the slope of the road. He takes a few strides toward her, squats and offers his hand.

"I'm very sorry, Miss Payne," he says, with a grin that makes him a liar. "I didn't mean to startle you."

She takes his hand and stands. Damn!

"Captain Auden, it is always lovely to see you."

"You're aiding in the search?"

"Nothing of the sort," she answers. "I am in the habit of leaving notes for several of my lovers around this old milestone, and they leave responses for me," she says, hoping to startle him back. She succeeds. The grin drops down to Auden's usual thin, straight line. He has a changeable face. Handsome, in most light. But it doesn't quite look like any other face. It wants studying.

Damn—her answer was too clever for her own good. She shouldn't have given anyone any reason to go ferreting around here. But Auden doesn't seem the prurient type. Curious, yes, but moral to a fault. He came home from the war around the same time Father did, bought New House and has been making a good go of it as a farmer.

He glances up the road toward the top of the hill. "I've been up and down this road in the night, and haven't found any signs of how our highwayman did away with two men and their carriage. Speaking of which, Miss Payne, I'd advise you not to ride out alone."

"I never am alone, if I can help it."

"Forgive me, but you're alone now."

"No, I'm not. I'm with you."

She really should learn to stop flirting. Jane doesn't mind it, but increasingly, Alice does. It doesn't feel fair anymore, not when she knows the people she's flirting with don't stand a chance. Not even handsome Captain Auden.

"Miss Payne, highwaymen might cut a romantic figure in stories, but I'm sure that they don't waste time on seduction if they meet a beautiful young woman on the road."

"Indeed? Well, I'm not too worried about that. Generally I'm the one doing the seducing, anyway."

He rolls his eyes, throws up his hands, and there's the grin again. Yes, that face is a study. If she did not have Jane in her life, she would like to run her fingertips over those hollows in his cheeks, that scar just beside his nose.

He didn't have that scar when he went to fight in America. He didn't have that limp either, the reason he came home.

"Well, if our highwayman has any brains," he says, "he'll stay away from these roads for a while now."

"You really believe the highwayman has killed or abducted them?"

He sighs. "I can't imagine it's a coincidence that they were robbed mere moments before."

"But it must be a coincidence. Why on earth would a highwayman rob a man, then go away, then, after being seen, ride back to that man to kill him? And spirit his carriage away?"

As much as she has hated each of the rapists and wife-beaters she has robbed, she has never contemplated killing any of them.

"Perhaps the servant, Grigson, chased the highwayman back onto the road. The man was startled, desperate, frightened. Hemmed in. He acted."

"And then spirited the carriage away."

"Drove it into a pond or something of that nature," says Auden, uncertainly. "That's my guess."

"Leaving no tracks on the road."

He cocks his head. "I didn't know you were a bloodhound as well as a natural philosopher, Miss Payne."

"Oh, I'm no philosopher. That's Jane Hodgson, my

companion. The contents of her study would rival Isaac Newton's. All kinds of machinery and instrumentation."

"How fascinating! Perhaps someday she might show it to me."

"Perhaps." She doesn't like this turn of the conversation. She and Jane have dangerous secrets, and it is not Alice's place to expose any of them.

"Well," Auden says, looking at the hedges, "if I don't find them today, I'll have to alert the magistrate. There will be many nervous people in London. The Bow Street Runners have started running patrols far outside the city. I imagine they'll come into this area now, if we've had a murder. And then there won't be much for a parish constable to do."

"Nor a highwayman," says Alice, looking down the road where so many of her odious marks have ridden.

"No," he says.

She glances up at him, and there's that grin again, but his eyes are serious.

"Shall I escort you home, Miss Payne?"

She shakes her head. "I would not dream of keeping a constable from his duty. If I meet the highwayman, I'll offer to ride away with him as his bride, and he'll be so frightened he'll leave England for good."

Auden laughs loudly. If he came home much changed

from the war, his changes are not the same as Father's.

She watches him ride off down the road to join the other men, and then she turns Havoc for home. Jane must have a look at the thing Alice took out of the daisy patch. If it isn't hers, perhaps she'll know what it is. She has never yet met a clock she couldn't repair. If the thing has gears, she'll make it do her bidding.

CHAPTER EIGHT

A Quarrel Ends in Silence

2070

IT TAKES A LOT to surprise a teleosopher, but Grace's words do it. Prudence looks around the tent, cluttered although she could count the items in it before she ran out of breath, and then catches herself. Grace catches her too.

"Yeah, I know. Who would have a baby, here and now?"

Prudence shrugs. "Lots of people do. Those tire swings and sand pits are out there for somebody."

"There's no work. There are too many people. But you know, maybe we could find a better time. An earlier time. Save up enough to all go, the three of us."

Prudence nods. "Sure. People do that."

The first refugees wanted the comfort of community. They wanted to be in a time when people knew about the existence of shimmering, when they would be understood. So they shimmered upstream only by one hundred years. But there are too many of them in this century, and no work, and drought-pricing is coming. And it costs a great deal for a civilian to shimmer.

Grace stands up, takes Prudence's empty plate and her own over to the bucket.

"It's a foolish idea. It's just what comes of us both being nearly forty now."

"Are we?" The words come out of Prudence's mouth. She kept track of the years pretty well during the Rudolf Project, but her own age feels a bit muddled.

"Yes, we are." Her sister grins. "Although I meant Alexei and me, but you're just a year behind. It might be easier to keep track of the birthdays if you spent some with us."

Prudence nods. "I have a chart. In my diary. But I'm behind on keeping it up."

Grace scratches one ear. "Yeah. Your diary. I wanted to ask you something about that."

Here it comes. The one question she fears from Grace: Do I always exist?

"You always said you had no interest in reading my diary." The words come out more sharply than Prudence intends. Grace did always say this, although "always" is something Prudence can't quite understand, no matter how many years she does this job. She can't understand how Grace has always said she didn't want to read her diary, while most of Prudence's diary was written by an only child.

"I don't," Grace snaps. "I don't want to know anything about myself. But if you know something about—about my child. If I have a child."

Prudence shakes her head and leans back on the cushion.

"I can honestly say I don't know anything about that," she says.

Grace looks at her, aware that there is a reason Prudence is hiding behind the technical truth, trying to decide if she wants to ask about that reason, aware that Prudence is aware that Grace is aware.

Grace nods, and scrubs the plates.

"We don't travel to all of the future," Prudence says, weakly. "Only bits, here and there. I spend most of my upstream time in 1889 and my downstream time down in 2145, where Command is, and it's all Anarchy then. After we left. Your child would be just a few years down from where we are now, or even further upstream, if you save enough to shimmer, right? So I wouldn't know."

Grace nods again.

"I can check some records," Prudence says. "It's against regulations, and there's no guarantee history will stay the same, but . . ."

Grace shakes her head. "I don't want to get you in trouble."

Prudence stands, goes outside to the privy. The conversation's over. In two more days, there won't be a diary to argue over, or any chance of Grace vanishing. Time's arrow will straighten, consequence will follow cause. If Grace has a child, it will live and die a child of the twenty-first century. Without a way to change the past, perhaps that child's generation will make a better future. No Anarchy, no History War. Just the long walk forward.

CHAPTER NINE

A Quarrel Ends in Adventure

1788

JANE'S TEA IS COLD, a sure sign that she's absorbed in a good puzzle. Alice puts the cold cup onto her tray and replaces it with a hot cup. The bread from this morning is gone, at least—a good sign.

The dim garret study is packed floor to ceiling with wooden arms and legs, rubber tubing, alembics and orreries. Alice tries to keep track of the food she's brought Jane, because it will often go weeks uneaten, tumbling behind some contraption, smelling and bringing mice. Of course, Jane never minds—she traps the mice in cages, and studies their habits.

She turns to go, but Jane says, "Stop a moment, Alice. I think I have this."

"Truly? It looked so complicated."

"Well, I suspect it *is* complicated, but the complicated

matter is under these smooth black pieces. Once I had them off, I could not understand the innards at all. Miniature machines of some kind. But once they are connected, all together, then the wheels do seem to have an effect. They are marked, you see? Tiny lines. If I arrange the nine wheels into the same pattern as when you found the device, and I depress this lever . . ."

Jane holds out the device and the air in the middle of the room shimmers in a circle, and suddenly the study smells like rain and wet pavement.

"What have you done?" Alice asks. "What is this?"

"It isn't magic. But whatever science it is, it's far beyond my knowledge. Watch."

Jane opens the door of a cage and pulls out a little grey mouse. She holds its nose to hers for a moment, whispers something, then puts the creature onto the floor and gives it a nudge toward the shimmering air.

The mouse crawls forward, and then it vanishes, not all at once but in a wave from nose to tail.

"Good Lord."

"Yes," says Jane, frowning. "Poor Cicero. I don't think he'll come back. I've been tossing bits of bread in all morning, and they do not reappear anywhere, from what I can see. And I watched a beetle walk in an hour ago. Oh, have they found the earl?"

Alice smiles. Jane's mind works in mysterious ways.

"They have not. Jane, do you think this device could make a carriage and three men vanish?"

"Yes, that has to be our hypothesis, I'm afraid. But what it's done to them, precisely, I can't say. Does it shrink matter to a very small size, or does destroy it utterly?"

"Look!" Alice cries out, and points to the floor, where three drops of liquid have fallen. "Is it rain? I believe it is. If it's taken our mouse, it's given us rain. I can smell it. It is some sort of window!"

And if that means Lord Ludderworth is not dead, perhaps he can be brought back, and his adventures explained, and the Bow Street Runners will not occupy themselves with this part of Hampshire, and the Holy Ghost will be free to ply her trade and keep her roof overhead.

"But no device can bring a person from one place to another with no connexion in between," protests Jane.

"No device you've seen, but this mechanism is entirely new and mysterious to you. You've said so."

Alice stands and walks around the disc of shimmering air, looking at it from one side and the other.

Jane kneels and puts her finger to the damp spot on the floor, sniffs it.

Alice says, "I'll have to go through."

"Alice! Didn't you see what happened to my mouse?"

"No, I didn't, in fact. I only saw one side of what happened to him. Lord Ludderworth and his men could be in danger, Jane."

"Then perhaps we should show this to Captain Auden." Jane looks uncertain.

"And have him take it from us? Before you know what it is, or how to use it?"

Jane frowns. She doesn't want to lose control of this machine any more than Alice does. But Jane won't dive in. Alice will.

Alice stands before the shimmering disc and thrusts her face into it.

It feels like the time she touched Jane's Leyden jar; it feels like the first time she touched Jane. Every part of her face tingles, almost painfully, and she can see a dim outline of a carriage and feel the rain on her face—

Jane pulls her back, gasping, tears welling in her cheeks.

"What in the Devil's name do you think you're doing? Your face vanished!"

"Yes," says Alice, grinning, excitement in her breast. "And look, here it is, still, just as it was! I'm going through. Look, don't you see that this proves that I will return? That it is another place? I saw rain, and a carriage!"

Jane puts one finger between her brows and draws one

breath. Then, "You did not even ask me, first. You could have been destroyed. And you could have destroyed this machine, this machine we know nothing about, a machine that is clearly an invention of great importance. You don't care what happens to anyone. You don't think about the future, only the present moment. Like a child."

"Jane—"

"I am not going to spend my life being nothing more than a useful companion and maker of amusements. I have spent all morning on this, and you stick your head through it like an oaf."

"Listen. My love. I am sorry, but nothing has been destroyed. I have shown that I can go through."

"Even so. There could be anything, anyone, on the other side. You might come out in Trafalgar Square, or in the jungles of Borneo."

Alice sighs. "I'll bring a knife, then. In case it's Trafalgar Square."

Jane's mouth is set. "I do not wish to be your assistant, Alice."

She says it as if she is turning away a bowl of turtle soup in a tavern. Jane has never been good at turning a phrase the expected way, or speaking it in the expected tone. It was one reason her mother was glad to send her to Alice, sociable Alice, who did not care in the least if her invitations to balls were out of curiosity or a taste for the exotic, and who dazzled every company.

They did not change each other, not in the way that Jane's mother hoped. But Alice is transformed, not by Jane herself but by her love for Jane, by her desire to keep something private and safe.

She steps around the shimmering air and enfolds Jane in her arms. She whispers into her golden wisps around her perfect ear, "Wherever it is, be it Fairyland or Lilliput or Hades, I'll come back to you. I must go, for our own protection. I have no intention of hanging for murders I did not commit, or even for the thefts I did. And if the Bow Street Runners start patrolling these roads, I'll have no choice but to hang up my mask and hat and be a good girl with no inheritance but Father's debts. And then what will become of us? Your mother will marry you to whatever lout can offer five hundred pounds."

Jane steps away from her, but her face is calm. "Then I'll go with you."

Alice laughs, and puts her hand over her mouth to stop it.

"What, is it so outrageous an idea, that I would go somewhere, do something, other than wait here in Fleance Hall for you to return from adventures?"

"It's not outrageous. It's wonderful. But I need you here, on guard, should Father and the search party return."

Jane sighs. "All right. I'll wait, as I always do. But you aren't going through the gateway here."

"No?"

"If the earl's carriage is indeed on the other side, and it comes back through, I would rather not have four horses and three men in my study."

Alice laughs again. "I would be lost without you. Come on then, let me get into my disguise, just in case I do find the earl, and we'll go out to the field."

CHAPTER TEN

Of Time and Space, with Four Horses

2070

HOW DOES A TRAVELLER find her way in a function-ally infinite map of four dimensions? The question plagued the early teleosophic researchers in the 2070s. It was one thing to find a way to find the permeable connections between all points in space-time; it was another to understand what those coordinates might mean, held up against the warp and weft of human history.

In the latest draft of that history, it was Fatima Sesay who discovered, and gave her name to, the Sesay Beacons. (An early entry in Prudence's diary describes these as the Yamamura Beacons.) Like their forebears, the humans of the twenty-second century looked to celestial events for guidance.

All events create gravitational ripples. Some create

tsunamis, and each of these gravity storms is unique. By matching the observed supernovae of history to the shape of space-time, the early time travellers were able to grope their way, as if each gravitational event were a beacon.

From there they filled in the map, down to the minute and the centimetre.

Five thirty in the morning on June 29, 2070, is rainy and grey. There's an alley behind the Toronto town house where not even raccoons or junkies meander at this hour. This is where Prudence drinks her coffee, out of a mug that says WORLD'S BEST DAD, wearing her eighteenth-century redingote.

If any one of the beacons were to become unrecognizable, the map would become useless. Prudence had a teacher who wired seven lights in a series, and showed how the whole line went dark when one was removed. Time travel would still be possible, but no one would know how to get anywhere. They'd be reduced to the same dangerous experiments that led to the discovery of the prehistory coordinates.

Some of the beacons are particularly subtle in their signatures. Particularly vulnerable to being changed, or obscured.

If need be, she will do the 1788 job herself, or give it a good try. To replace the beacon with an ever-changing random set of electromagnetic pulses and render space-time unnavigable. Stop the History War before it begins.

But Helmut is right about the causality glitch. Paradoxes don't cause as much trouble as the early teleosophers feared. Still, actually taking some action in a period that makes one's own journey to that period impossible is tricky. Ugly things can happen. People can get stuck in a kind of limbo between times, and the action itself can take on a kind of quantum uncertainty, so that the evidence a hundred years afterward can contradict itself about what actually happened.

This will be true of pushing the button, or of setting a timer. Any human choice seems to carry causality risk. A human choice of this magnitude is not something to play around with.

So to be as safe as possible, they need a person to press the button in 1788—a person who will stay in 1788, who has not shimmered there.

She puts the coffee mug on the ground and readies herself. She isn't using her shimmer belt today, because she couldn't find a way to hide it in clothing of this period. She is carrying a portable shimmer in her hand, a lovely brass time-wheel.

She presses the lever. A change in the smell of the air, a glancing beam of sunlight so bright it makes her eyes water.

She steps through the shimmer, into England in 1788, off to find Jane Hodgson. Onto a hill near a road, a short walk from Fleance Hall.

She takes one step through and hesitates. She hears horses nearby—on the road, they must be. Hoofbeats and the rattle of a carriage.

The sky darkens.

She steps back.

Something smacks into her and she falls, her head hits the asphalt. Horse hoofs hammering. Pain shattering her hand. She screams and rolls to one side, out of the way of the horses.

Horses. Horses? Did the shimmer open on the road? Perhaps her calculations were off. Shit.

Shit.

They're in 2070, in the alley, these horses. And the carriage behind them. If it weren't for the pain in her hand, she could think—

The man driving the horses shouts something, and yanks on the reins and the horses stand, tossing their heads and flaring their nostrils.

She whimpers with pain.

The carriage door opens and a man tumbles out. All silk and buttons and powder, and a face like a pug's, trusting and uncertain.

"What is this?" he sputters, looking right at her, at the

piss-stinking alley walls and trash cans. "What sort of trick?"

"Hi!" the coachman yells. "There's a woman down there! Madam, are you hurt?"

Then an arm comes around his neck and someone's pulling him down, off the seat, and holding a pistol to the footman's head. A third person up on the carriage seat, a masked person in a tricorne hat and grey cloak. Like someone in a highwayman costume.

Like a highwayman.

Mother of all that's holy, what rotten luck is this?

The footman pushes the pistol and leaps down to the ground, and something flashes. A knife? There's metal at the coachman's throat.

"Stop!" Prudence screams.

CHAPTER ELEVEN

How the Earl Is Rescued

2070

ALICE, DRESSED AS THE Holy Ghost and with her dagger in hand, runs along the side of Lord Ludderworth's gaudy carriage in a strange dim alley in the rain. She grabs the footboard and pulls herself up onto the coachman's seat.

All these months, she has avoided getting this close to any of the carriages she's robbed. Wherever she is, she is here without Laverna, without any help.

"Drive backward!" she yells, but the coachman doesn't hear her. He's standing, looking at the ground on the far side. "Get the carriage out of this place!"

"Hi!" the coachman yells. "There's a woman down there! Madam, are you hurt?"

Someone pushes her—the footman—she stumbles, nearly falls off the driver's seat. The footman is reaching for something. Before she can think too hard about it, she's got the pistol at the footman's temple and is pulling the dagger out from behind her busk and placing it at the coachman's throat, screaming at him to get down.

There is indeed a woman on the ground, a black woman but in a redingote of good quality, if it is a few years out of date.

"Stop!" she yells. She is holding her hand to her chest and squirming on the ground.

Nothing to be done about her at the moment. Alice forces the coachman onto his arse on the seat. The footman stands there watching, holding onto the bar as if the carriage were moving.

The stranger moans. She's in pain, holding her hand—the horses must have trampled her. But she doesn't seem to be in any real danger.

Alice pauses, glances around. It's an ugly place, bricked in and stinking, full of strange-looking pipes and wire fences. Something like a slaughterhouse.

She'll investigate, after she gets the three men back to where they ought to be.

"I'll be happy to assist you, madam," Alice says, "after this carriage goes back through the—through to where it is supposed to be."

A hand grabs her pistol and wrenches her arm backward. Damn these thickheaded men! She stumbles down off the carriage and drops the pistol but does not fall, and she elbows her captor right in the pudding, turns around to see who it is.

It's the Earl of Ludderworth. He bends over, groaning.

"What in the Devil's name do you think you're doing?" she screams at him.

"You won't do my coachman any harm," he gasps. "We paid your price. Now let us go. I don't know what kind of trick this is, but you will set us free or I will see you hang."

"Set you free? You addlepate, I'm rescuing you!"

He swings his fist at her, not even coming close to connecting.

"Oh no you don't, my lord. Someone's setting me up to hang for your murder, and I think we'd both rather that didn't come to pass."

She pricks his back with her dagger and he stumbles forward, but she doesn't have time to march him through the gate. The coachman is clambering off his perch, and the strange woman is at the heads of the horses, walking around them to her.

Alice pushes Lord Ludderworth hard so that he stumbles toward the back of the carriage and disappears into the shimmering air. She turns to face the coachman. He's got a rapier in his hand, the fool.

She waits until he thrusts it forward, aimed at her

shoulder, then she ducks to the side, whirls and stabs the
back of his knee with her dagger. His scream pierces the
air and he falls flat on his face.

She puts her dagger in her belt and grabs him by the
wrists, drags him backward and then kicks him so that he
rolls through the window.

He disappears after his master.

The footman runs after them.

She turns again, and there is the stranger, holding
some kind of weapon. It is nothing like a pistol, but it is
very definitely pointed at Alice.

Alice holds up her hands to show that they're empty.
"I'm going to try to have the horses walk the carriage
back through the gate now. It's a rather shabby carriage
despite the gaudy paint and the horses are terribly old.
Not very valuable. I give you my word that I'll replace the
cost of what you've stolen here, and a little extra besides.
There is honour among thieves, isn't there? I have heard
people say that, although I've never known quite what
they meant."

The stranger only raises her eyebrows.

Alice decides to take that as assent, and walks gingerly
past her to the horses. They are terrified, but as she
pushes gently on the harness, they step back. It doesn't
take much, then, only a push, and the horses walk the
carriage back through the aura. It disappears into it, bit

by bit, like the mouse. The last thing she sees are the faces of the horses, unaware of the disappearance of their hindquarters.

She and the strange woman are alone in the alley.

CHAPTER TWELVE

Shit Gets Weird; or, a
Consequential Encounter

2070

THE PERSON IN THE CLOAK and tricorne hat leans Misguided by temperament, but not heavily enough to be an agent. Not a teleosopher, then; a naïf. A civilian, from 1788.

This much Prudence has gleaned from the EEG scanner, which could no doubt tell her more if it were not programmed with the needs of a teleosophic military operative in mind. But at the moment, Prudence cares very little about this person's ideology.

Her hand, at least, doesn't seem to be broken, now that she's had a chance to wiggle it. It still stings but the hoof seems to have just caught the edge of her flesh. A bad bruise, that's all.

"I'm not a thief," Prudence says, at last. "You are, though, I take it."

"I am in a mask, and we are not at a ball."

Prudence shrugs. "All right. Well, I can tell you that I have nothing worth stealing, and if you'll walk back the same way you sent the carriage . . ."

"Your accent is strange. You weren't born in England. Are you escaping your master? I can take you to some Quakers I know."

A face appears at a window, behind bars, a little way down the alley. An angry, suspicious face. Shit. Four terrified horses and three terrified men make too much fucking noise. This is a disaster.

"I don't need your help, thank you. You should do as you urged those men to do, and go that way. It's all an illusion—a trick of *electricity*."

She expects the word *electricity* to produce a frisson of delighted horror in 1788, but the highwayman makes no movement and if there's an expression behind the mask and kerchief, Prudence can't see it.

"I'm not going anywhere until you tell me where we are."

She was going to 1788 to get a naïf. She wanted Jane Hodgson, but a highwayman who is evidently very clever and very reckless will do nicely. And a highwayman will be likely to be greedy.

All right, then. Any teleosopher knows how to roll with change.

"We are in the Americas." Truth! Always the best option.

The person in the tricorne hat whistles softly, but stands very still, only moving their head a bit to glance back toward the portal. The next question—*when are we*—trumpets in Prudence's mind. But the person in the tricorne hat does not voice it. Does not think it, almost certainly.

It's almost disappointing. It is such an exhilaration, to shimmer from one moment of space-time to another. Like the body's shudder between waking and sleeping. To think that someone could be one of the few humans ever to experience that, and not know it for what it is—but it is for the best. Prudence's concern now is to cause the fewest ripples downstream, before she brings the tsunami.

"And why did you open this wonderful gateway to England?"

"I need someone to do something for me," Prudence says, "in England, at a very specific time. And that someone will be richly rewarded."

The cloaked person turns and looks at the shimmer, still open. "How does it work?"

"I can't tell you that."

"Hmm. And if I want that knowledge as my reward?"

"The reward is fifty thousand pounds. In gold." She watches to see the effect. It's hard to tell with a mask, but the person moves, steps back slightly as if in shock.

"And what do you demand of me?"

"Nothing that will break the laws of England."

The stranger waits.

"It won't kill anyone or steal any goods," Prudence says, taking refuge in the literal truth for the second time that day. Why does she find it so difficult to lie? She was trained to believe in every word she said, as a propagandist. Perhaps she doesn't know anymore how to be anything but an honest liar. No one is wrong, the Farmers' creed declared. Only misguided.

"Will it affect my life at all?"

"Not in the slightest. But I won't tell you what it is unless you show me your face and give me your name."

The highwayman stands, as if considering.

"I'll think on it," the highwayman says. "If I go back through the portal, how can I find you again?"

"I'll open a portal to the same spot, by Dray Road, tomorrow." Tomorrow for the highwayman, and tomorrow for Prudence. If the highwayman comes back, having decided to do the job, Prudence will keep them here in 2070 until the right moment. And if they don't, she'll still have time tomorrow to go back and try to find Hodgson.

She needed a naïf. She got one. Everything will be fine.

The highwayman steps back through the portal, leaving Prudence standing in the alley alone, trying to determine exactly why she's so uneasy.

CHAPTER THIRTEEN

In Which Alice Is Discombobulated

1788

ALICE STEPS THROUGH THE GATEWAY and sees the faces of the horses again. Why do they tarry? The coachman and the footman are scrambling onto the seat.

Someone grabs her arm. Alice turns, knife in hand, but it's Jane. Jane pulls her after her, running, and through a break in the yew hedge that marks the edge of Fleance Hall's gardens and the beginning of its fields. They peer at the carriage. The earl is shouting "Go, go!" and the coachman has the horses in hand now, if not himself.

"They came through the moment you went in," whispers Jane. "Why did you come with them? Was it not safe to stay?"

Alice frowns. "Stay? I thought you would be worried if I stayed longer. But I've been invited back."

The carriage wheels around and rattles over the dry

field toward the track that leads to Fleance Hall's stables. Three of its lanterns are still lit.

Jane steps back, frowns deeper. "You mean to say you met someone? But you were only there a moment. Three seconds, at most, between your disappearance and your appearance."

Alice shakes her head. "I don't understand. It was an alley. It was in America. I spoke with someone—a woman. She wants me to—"

"Alice, you were gone a mere moment. Ten seconds at most."

The carriage rolls slowly on the dry field, rollicking as it goes, as the coachman pushes the horses faster than he should. Back toward Fleance Hall.

"We must get back," says Jane. "Your father will want us, once the earl arrives."

Alice nods and takes her hand. They run back, taking the shadows along the hedge, darting to the servants' door.

As they undress and re-dress Alice, she relates her conversation with the stranger.

"Fifty thousand pounds!" breathes Jane.

"It would set us up for life, with a bit of good management. We can pay Father's debts, restore Fleance Hall to what it ought to be. No more shooting and gambling parties with Father's disagreeable friends. We'll hold salons, and invite Olaudah Equiano and the Duchess of Devonshire and Fanny Burney, and we will definitely not invite Dr. Johnson or Edmund Burke. Oh, and we'll finance the campaigns of all the best Whigs, and get slavery abolished and democracy rooted. And we'll build that little cottage with clematis and roses, but we won't need it because you and I will be mistresses of Fleance Hall and too rich to care what anyone says about it."

Jane smiles, raising her eyebrows. She pulls a pin out of her mouth, which gives her a chance to get a word in.

"It is a pretty fancy. But how can any of it be true?"

"We saw the truth of the gateway, at least, with our own eyes."

"Did we?" Jane asks, wearing her puzzled face. "While you were talking, I have been thinking about the difference in the time . . ."

"Of course. You never listen to me. I don't blame you."

"And I think perhaps it could be more than just a gateway to America. It could be a gateway to another time."

"Another . . . time."

"That would explain it, you see? It is sunset on June twenty-ninth on one side of the portal, and some other date and time on the other, so when you came back through, it was still sunset at June twenty-ninth. The markings on the concentric wheels of the device must be like the lines on a compass, a guide of some kind."

Alice, for once, has no words. "Do you think it is possible?"

Jane, for once, smiles. "No. But what else would explain it?"

As Alice sucks in her breath so Jane can pin her bodice closed, it begins to seem an invention of her mind from start to finish. How could any of it be true?

She pulls Lord Ludderworth's purse out from under the loose floorboard and transfers his coins to a small reticule of her own.

"In any event," she says, "I suppose we shall learn more tomorrow."

"Tomorrow? You don't mean to go back to this stranger and accept her commission?"

"Well, no," says Alice, discombobulated. "Well, possibly. We must learn more about what all this is, and how else can we—I mean, I won't do what she asks, unless it seems wise. But it is too soon to prejudge."

"To prejudge! How could it possibly seem wise? What evidence could one possibly duplicitous stranger give you, in one day, to make you return to her and carry out her instructions, whatever they may be? She will likely be waiting with a group of Bow Street Runners. You have only her word to suggest she was in America."

Jane is looking at her as if she is stupid. Jane, who cannot see past the bridge of her nose, who looks at the world through spectacles and lenses and bottles.

"There may be a risk in inaction too," says Alice, low and soft like a purr or a growl. Less than an hour ago, Jane was in a snit about not being consulted enough, and here she is making up her mind for both of them, and acting as if Alice is a child for considering all possibilities.

If she wanted to, Jane could go home, and her mother would forgive her for being unsatisfactory, and even if she never married, she would at least have a roof overhead for the rest of her days. Alice does not have that choice. No one will take care of Alice if she does not take care of herself. She cannot turn away the offer of fifty thousand pounds as if it were nothing.

Jane is shaking her head. "Sometimes I think you see me as a great experiment, that you say things to get satisfaction from my shock. Little Jane, poor and plain, small bubbies and a big brain. That's what the boys used to say, to shock me. You could try it, rather than declaring your intention to disappear into some other time and place and carry out some unknowable scheme at a stranger's behest."

Alice feels her cheeks heat, and she blinks from surprise. "That I see you as an experiment! You! Who can't understand a thing unless it is struggling in one of your cages, impaled on one of your pins!"

Jane turns and walks out of the study. As Alice follows,

down the garret staircase, she hears Father's voice, and the earl's.

They're here.

Jane is at the bottom of the staircase now, and she turns and heads in the direction of the front of the house, where the drawing room is. She must know full well this means Alice will have to hang back and wait, so that they don't seem to arrive together. There is nothing to raise suspicion in a woman and her companion being together, but Alice and Jane have gotten into the habit of making separate entrances nevertheless. If anyone in either of their families guessed the truth about them, everything would be over. They'd never see each other again.

Alice waits, and listens to Jane's voice raised in polite greeting. She curses under her breath and strides into the drawing room herself.

The room seems full of men, all standing, all drinking. There are two in the Ludderworth livery, sickly green and gold. There is Father, at the decanter, and Lord Ludderworth himself, a glass of port shaking at his lips.

"Alice," Father says, turning. "Look, Lord Ludderworth is safe. And his men too."

She strides forward. Auden is there too, watching her, his hat in his hands.

And there's the coachman who gave her so much trouble.

"And Mr. . . . ." she says, looking at the coachman.

"Mr. Greenleaf, at your service, Miss Payne. And this is Mr. Jones, footman."

She nods, and then inclines her head to Ludderworth. He has put down his glass, holds out his hand, so she gives him hers. His whiskers brush the top of it.

"Miss Payne."

"Well, you must tell me the solution to the mystery," she says brightly. "Did your carriage run off the road?"

Ludderworth shakes his head. "We were taken, through some abominable trickery. One moment we were on the road, and the next, we were in an alley. And with us, a woman, pretending that we knocked her down. An accomplice of the highwayman, I have no doubt. He was there too."

She glances at Auden, who is looking at her more intently than he ought. Good; he's giving her a reason for her blush.

"An alley!" says Jane.

"Bricks and all," groans Ludderworth. "And there, the highwayman attacked us again, and pushed us back the way we came. Then, in the twinkling of an eye, there we were in your father's fields, with no alley to be seen."

"It was night," says Jane. "And there was a great deal of confusion, I'm sure, after you were set upon."

"I know what I saw, Miss Hodgson," says Greenleaf. "Begging your pardon."

"And it was not night when we came out, although we had only been in a few minutes," says Ludderworth.

"Best not to tell these men they've imagined things until we've heard the whole story, eh, Jane?" barks Father.

Jane blushes and looks down at her hands. And now Auden is looking at Jane, not with the same intensity as he looked at Alice but with a frown, as though he is trying to make sense of her. Good luck to him!

Alice tries to catch Jane's eye. Damn Father. He was never abrupt with people, before. Jane knows his ways well enough but it is one thing to put up with it in private, and quite another in front of visitors. She'll feel even more like a servant, an appendage, undervalued.

"Jane is only applying science," Alice says, smiling. But Jane does not look at her.

"Science indeed," growls Ludderworth. "It was an electric device of some kind, I feel sure, that moved us from one place to another. First the automaton, now this. This is no ordinary highwayman but an inventor bent upon using his machines to commit crimes. We will need a full investigation so that Her Majesty's government can pass the appropriate laws."

"To begin with, perhaps we can apply our reason to

the problem," says Auden. "Perhaps there is a secret entrance to a brick structure of some kind. A tunnel, perhaps. You stumbled into the highwayman's lair, and he, desperate, attacked you and pushed you out."

"But then where is this place?" Father asks, leaning forward.

"Damned if I know," says Auden, and glances again at Jane, who stands at one end of the room, and then at Alice, who is on the other. "My apologies, Miss Payne, Miss Hodgson."

Alice grins at him.

But he is looking past her, and does not smile back. "Perhaps," he muses, "there is some device nearby. A wire, or lever, and a horse kicked it and opened the secret gate. I will take a hound over that part of the road."

"But you've done so already," says Alice. "Surely you would have found it."

"Then what is your explanation, Miss Payne?" Auden asks.

"My explanation?" She blinks, tries to focus on his face, his fascinating, ever-shifting face. She would like to watch it move for hours; she would like to freeze a single expression on it.

"Miss Payne, you have said that Miss Hodgson inclines to a scientific view. What is yours, then? Surely you don't believe that the Earl of Ludderworth and Mr.

Greenleaf and Mr. Jones all drove into Fairyland."

She smiles. "Oh, I am sure Jane's approach is the right one. But Jane has taught me that a good natural philosopher never discounts any possibility, Captain Auden."

He raises his eyebrows. "Well, if I am to find any clews on the road, I should be at it. Thank you for the port, Colonel Payne. It is lucky I was passing when Lord Ludderworth arrived. Poor Grigson is still out beating the bushes with the two footmen, so I will find them to give them the news. I trust you will be comfortable here, my lord, and Mr. Greenleaf and Mr. Jones. May I call upon you again if I have fresh questions?"

"Of course," says Ludderworth. "I'll make my excuses now too, if I might, Colonel, and Miss Payne. My men and I have not slept, and it seems we should have."

She bows her head and drops a small curtsy, and Satterthwaite steps forward to take the overdue guests to their rooms. Jane leaves the room before Alice can even catch her eye.

CHAPTER FOURTEEN

On the Limits of Patience

2145

PRUDENCE STEPS INTO 2145 and sees General Almo more or less where she left him, at his desk, the lights on his display table glimmering and shifting. It's been perhaps two minutes here—long enough for one portal to close and another to open—while she's spent a day in 2070.

"Well?" he asks. "How are you finding it? No changes at this end, yet, but I don't expect any after one day."

She nods, hopes she looks like a team player. "It's a long game this time, General. I've published the books but we'll need other changes to reinforce them or they'll choir-preach. So I've connected with a couple of young people who will be involved in the 2091 Berlin Convention. Radical Misguided converts. Helmut Kauffmann and Rati Kapoor. If I change their life plans, they won't meet Tremblay next year. Trying to seed events but also steering them away from activism to avoid stream-correction. The changes might take a bit of work before they show up."

Her connection with Rati and Helmut might be visible to him; there must be some record of the apartment in their name, of her presence on the security cameras. And indeed, if she hadn't come into their lives, Rati and Helmut would have become leaders in the movement to broaden access to manufactured organs, which would eventually have led to the disintegration of the household model of taxation and to the obsolescence of civil marriage. The Misguideds have agents at the Berlin Convention working to strengthen the declaration and polarize public opinion, so the Farmers are trying to head them off by working before 2091.

The thing that none of the Farmers will admit is that all their work only stretches the dialectic to greater extremes, accelerating the pace of the very change they're trying to stop, and pushing it in directions the Misguideds don't want it to go. History doesn't self-correct in response to an attack; it metastasizes.

The general has his own version of a diary, but unlike laypeople, he doesn't need to keep it in prehistory to keep it from changing. It's a new technology, one that Prudence doesn't understand. Somehow, the general's display table exists in a bubble of space-time. Its energy costs don't bear thinking about.

"Major Zuniga," he says, not looking up from the table, "you have family in 2070, don't you?"

He knows full well she does.

"My sister."

During the long moment in which he does not answer, looking at his table, she wills him not to say *What sister?* Every time she shimmers, she thinks: perhaps this is the moment it all changes.

But instead he says, "Do what you must, but remember that you'll spend weeks of your life on this, even if it passes in a blink of an eye from my perspective. I need you young and healthy and there is so much work to do. If history won't nudge in the direction you want in Toronto in 2070, I'll redeploy you somewhere else. 'Our patience will achieve more than our force.'"

"Edmund Burke?"

"Exactly." General Almo looks up at her. "Report back tomorrow. I'll be here." His mouth curls at the joke, a sign that he still has faith in her, that he's giving her more slack than she deserves.

She nods and salutes, spending a moment longer than she should taking in one of the few sights that have been a constant for her last ten years: his big shoulders, belly running just slightly to paunch pressing against the grey regulation T-shirt, perfect shave still leaving a shadow on his golden skin, close-curled hair going grey at the temples. If all goes according to plan, she'll never see this man again.

CHAPTER FIFTEEN

A Complication Arises

1788

"**ALICE**," **FATHER SAYS**, just as she says, "Father."

He frowns. "I have important news."

She inclines her head. "Then you must speak first, of course."

"When Lord Ludderworth and his men first burst in upon me, before we sent for Captain Auden, His Lordship was distraught."

"As well he might be."

"Indeed, but what distressed him most was the idea that he might become a laughingstock, I think. That people might disbelieve his story, call him a drunkard or an idiot. And it soon became apparent that by 'people,' he chiefly meant you, Alice."

"Me!"

"Yes." Father takes both her hands in his. His face

is lit up by port or elation or some combination. "It seems he had intended on asking for your hand today. It came out of him as a kind of lament, but I assured him that not only would I have consented before, but that I do now."

Her hand! She is thirty-two now, and thought she was safe. The prospect of marriage evaporated when she was twenty-two years old, when Father went to war, and there was no one left to try to marry her off. Since his return, they had both seemed set on the project of ensuring that Alice could live at Fleance Hall comfortably until her death as an old maid.

Father's method of ensuring this is to speculate in shaky ventures in the Americas, and to drink when they fail. Alice has her own methods.

Marriage! And to Lord Ludderworth!

"He . . . he loves me?" she whispers.

"Indeed."

"But I do not love him."

"Alice, don't be a child. This will make you Countess of Ludderworth—to think, someone of your heritage being a countess!"

Your heritage, he says, as if her mother were some unfortunate accident that befell him. As if he stumbled.

"You'll gain not only a title—something we never considered in our wildest dreams—but money too. His

Lordship is a wealthy man. You'll have enough to keep Fleance Hall. Or you could sell it. I suppose you will have houses enough, and won't want this one."

"But I love Fleance Hall. It's all I want. I don't want to be countess of anything."

"Alice. You and I know full well that another opportunity will not come for you. No man of substance, and of lesser generosity of spirit than His Lordship, will look past your—"

"My skin? You must have looked past it, with my mother."

She sets her jaw. He never speaks of her mother, and the very mention makes his face redden.

"Alice, if you do not marry Lord Ludderworth, you won't get Fleance Hall when I die."

The words make no sense. She reorders them, and they still make no sense.

"I don't understand. The property is not entailed. It is not a family seat. You bought it outright. You can will it to whomever you wish."

"Indeed. And I will not leave it to you, unmarried, and with no fortune of your own to sustain you. Without a house of this size to maintain, without servants, you may find some work that will keep you from starving. I have raised you up to a higher class and colour, Alice, and if you insist on sinking back down again, you will do it without my participation."

She can barely hear over the drumbeat of her blood in her ears.

"Father," she bites, "you are an ignorant fool."

She almost thinks he will strike her. They stare at each other for a moment. Then, to her shock, he nods.

"Yes," he says, the thickness of shame in his voice. "I am. I have lost everything, Alice! I have tried to keep it from you, the worst of it, but I have many debts."

So quickly he changes, like the weather, from a pompous ass to a haunted shadow of the father she knew, the father whose confidences she held even as a little girl, whose respect was as dependable as Christmas.

If Father only knew how many times she has gone to his creditors, paid them what she could to keep him out of prison for another month or two, asked them to keep it silent from him. Her story is always that she sold her mother's rings. She never visits the same creditor twice, so she's running out of ways to stanch the bleeding without attracting notice.

She sighs, unties the reticule from her belt and hands it to him.

"Here," she says, more coldly than she intends. "I won a game of faro at Mrs. Thackeray's soiree the other night. You can put this toward some of the debts."

Father takes it and holds it in his hand, weighing it,

looking straight at her. Then he shuts his eyes tight, opens them again and pours the contents of the bag onto his hand. Lord Ludderworth's coins fill his open palm. She'll have to sell the rings and watch, when she gets a chance to send Jane to London.

"Your pardon."

They turn to see Wray Auden standing in the doorway. "I forgot my hat," he says, holding it up.

"How odd," says Jane, standing in the door.

How long has Jane been there, listening? Did she hear about the horrible proposal? Could she possibly think that Alice might consent to it? Her face is as still as stone. To the world, it wears no expression, but Alice can see it as anger. But anger over their argument, or something else? "I could have sworn you had it in your hand when you left."

Auden smiles. "The memory is an unreliable witness, as I am sure we will be reminded tomorrow when I question our poor victims some more. Good night, ladies, and Colonel."

Alice uses his departure as an excuse to go straight up the stairs without another word to her father, but Jane won't be caught. She goes into her bedroom and closes the door, and that has always been a signal between them. Alice stands in the corridor, her skirt in her hand, and thinks for a moment.

She needs to know more, and she needs to know it now. They have a device that can send them through time! Surely they can solve any problem that way. She can prevent Father from ever going to the war. She can find out whether she can keep collecting tolls as the Holy Ghost without Auden catching her.

But first, she can find out whether fifty thousand pounds is worth doing the bidding of a woman in America. She can find out—and here her brow tightens on its own, and she sniffs sharply, caught off guard by a sudden unmooring thought—she can find out who the woman is.

Jane spoke of the marks on a compass. If one were to move the lines from their current setting, just a little . . .

CHAPTER SIXTEEN

Concerning the Course of History; with Revelations

2070

PRUDENCE STEPS BACK THROUGH the portal, into her workroom in suburban Toronto in 2070, and for a moment can't process what she sees. A second portal is open just opposite.

Between the two portals stands the highwayman, pointing a pistol at Prudence's gut.

Prudence elbows the button at her waist and the portal closes behind her. She's seen experiments where teleosophic scientists shoot bullets through shimmers, and they do just exactly what you'd expect. If General Almo hears a bullet whirr past his ear, or worse, she'll be investigated. Project Shipwreck will never happen.

"Time," says the person in the highwayman costume, their face covered in a mask and kerchief. "It's time, isn't it?"

The shimmer's on the far side of her workroom, a perfect circle cutting through the chalkboard covered in equations. Her workroom doesn't smell quite right; there's something greasy or metallic, like her father's workroom in the basement of her childhood home.

"How did you get here?"

"I used the device you left behind, when the horses knocked you down. I tinkered with it a little."

Shit. Shit! Prudence pats her pocket, but of course it shouldn't be in this pocket but in the reticule with her eighteenth-century clothes.

But it isn't there. It's in the possession of an eighteenth-century highwayman.

Prudence can almost hear the gears in her own mind turning. This naïf, if they truly are a naïf, knows more than they should. All right. Then? Next.

"But it was not set to open here and now."

"I tinkered with it."

Prudence raises an eyebrow. The time-wheel is the sort of thing anyone could use without much knowledge, even if they don't use it well. The mechanical circles are deliberately simple and external, as a fail-safe, to make sure that the device will work only in a predictable way for a teleo even if the history of technology changes while the teleo is jumping.

The consequence, of course, is that anyone can work

it. But a naïf wouldn't know what the markings meant. They'd have to take a guess, and then walk through, hoping for the best.

The time-wheel has its fail-safes built in. Her plan needs a fail-safe too. The wheels turn: yes. Yes, this could work.

"Well, that was risky," she says. "Who the hell are you?"

"Madam, I am the one holding the gun."

Prudence shrugs. "Shoot me then. I'm not saying a word until I know who you are."

She crosses her arms across her chest, waits for the masks to come off. She doesn't know how reliable an eighteenth-century pistol might be, but at a two-foot range, it doesn't have to shoot straight or fast to cause a lot of pain.

The highwayman rips off the mask, and pulls down the green kerchief.

"I'm Alice Payne, daughter of Colonel Payne. I was born in 1756, in Jamaica, and I live in Hampshire now."

A woman. Explains the kerchief over the mask, which seemed like overkill. Explains a lot, really.

Prudence points at the two rickety office chairs. "Can we sit? You can keep that pointed at me if you want."

"Answer one question honestly, first."

Prudence nods and watches Alice get it ready: a slight frown, a quiver of the lip.

"You are my mother. Aren't you?"

The air comes out of Prudence, through her nose, a snort that sounds like a laugh but isn't, that makes Alice frown. Goddammit, that is not a question she ever expected from anyone.

"Your *mother*?"

"I didn't know her," Alice says.

"And you think . . . wait. Are there really so few black women where you're from, that you meet any random black lady, and you think, 'This must be my *mother*'?"

"You're not, then?"

"No. Definitely not. I'm sorry."

At least she now knows one thing: the EEG scanner was right. This woman is a genuine naïf, albeit a bright one. She's going to have to be a true recruit to the cause, then, not a patsy.

That's all right. Prudence can recruit people. She used to do quite a lot of it.

Alice frowns and gestures to the chairs by cocking her head. She keeps the pistol trained on Prudence as Prudence walks over and sits, then she takes the other chair. She spins out the truth, little by little, to see what it will hook.

"I'm Major Prudence Zuniga. Born in 2132."

The woman narrows her eyes. "You mean to say that anno Domini 2132 is through that gateway?"

She says it "two thousand one hundred and thirty-two" rather than "twenty-one thirty-two."

"Not quite," Prudence says. "I was coming from 2145. From Teleosophic Core Command. The headquarters of a military operation."

"The same military organization of which you are a major. A military organization that accepts women into its ranks, and as officers! For which country?"

"For no country. For an idea."

"Ah. A revolutionary."

"Not quite," says Prudence. "Down past 2139, the world's in Anarchy. Things went very, very wrong with humanity and with the planet itself. The present, my present, does not look salvageable. So the teleosophers—people who study the way that time travel changes history—started trying to fix the past."

"To change history. Truly?"

"Yes. We're in 2070 now, you know. My past. Your future."

The woman looks around, as if she might see some wonder in Prudence's particleboard furniture. She looks at Prudence, at her khakis and T-shirt.

The future must seem very drab to her. As it should.

"But soon enough," Prudence continues, "there was a difference of opinion about how to fix things. Those of us who remained under Teleosophic Core Command, the original organization, we're called Farmers. The others, those who went rogue, they call themselves Guides. They believe in a more aggressive approach."

"I don't know what that means."

Prudence switches on her marketing-copy brain.

"The Guides are not malicious. They're just wrong. They believe in the perfectibility of humanity. In progress. We call them the Misguideds. They try to speed up change, while we try to reverse humanity's mistakes."

"So you're a Tory," Alice says.

Prudence laughs. "Ha! I guess so, in one sense. I believe that there is a virtue in the status quo, and that change should be cautious and deliberate. A Tory. And the Misguideds would be—what is it in your time? Whigs?"

"Yes," says Alice. "I am a Whig."

"Ah." Shit.

"Well, everyone's a Whig nowadays. But I'm one of the ones you'd call radical, I suppose. I've published an anonymous essay against slavery. I believe in progress too, Major Zuniga. I am misguided, I suppose you would say."

Prudence should have trained better for the eighteenth century. She's going to have to get Alice on board, quickly.

She leans forward, lowers her voice, although there is no one here but them.

"It isn't what the Misguideds believe that makes them

my enemy. It's their actions. And, to be honest, the actions of my fellow Farmers too."

"I don't understand."

"I'm not working for the Farmers anymore. I'm secretly working to put an end to this war."

Alice frowns. "An end to war is a noble goal."

"Indeed. And our war—our war is the war that starts all wars. So much of the world you know is a consequence of our arrogance. We've changed the past. You are in the cross fire. You ever wonder where your King George got the nickname 'the Farmer'?"

Alice pulls a face. "Surely not."

"He's one of ours. One of these times around he'll stop the American Revolution entirely, and you won't know that history was ever any other way. He's been prolonging it . . ."

"Prolonging the American war?"

"Indeed."

Alice shakes her head. "Then I must support your goal, Major Zuniga. My father's service in that war has changed both our lives and brought me much grief. If you—but wait a moment. How do *you* know what's changed? If history is a certain way, and you're a product of that history, how do you remember how it was before?"

She *is* clever, this Alice Payne. More clever than most Farmer agents Prudence has worked beside.

Clever enough to be her own fail-safe, built in. Like the time-wheel. *With* the time-wheel. Good. That's what Prudence hoped for, from Jane Hodgson. Turns out there is more than one clever woman living in Fleance Hall in 1788.

"I don't remember the past being different," says Prudence lightly. "I can only remember things the way they are now, even if I didn't actually live through them that way. But I keep a diary in the Precambrian."

"Where?"

"A very long time ago, before any teleosophic interference. A lot of us do it. It's not a nice time to visit, but we have ways to protect ourselves while we're there. The diary is just paper, so no fool antiquarian can dig it up. There are smaller clues, though, clues we can't avoid, and we leave them all over like rabbits leave droppings. The more people time-travel, the earlier humanity discovers time travel, bit by bit, and the mess gets bigger."

Prudence makes an expanding motion with her hands, as if there's an explosion between her palms, and continues: "There are scholars trying to predict this effect through mathematics, and philosophers writing new treatises on something we call the dialectics of time travel. All from the safety of twenty years before the Anarchy, of course. From whenever the Anarchy happens to land at the time."

Alice shakes her head. "I still don't understand—well, there is very much I do not understand. But let's begin with why you opened a gateway on my road."

Her road. There's a clue in that; there's something Prudence might be able to use, if she can grok its significance.

"I need your help. Alice, if you'd like to protect your family, the people you love, even your England, from further harm, then the best thing you can do is carry out the instructions I mentioned at our last meeting. Everything I told you was true."

"But not the whole truth."

Prudence leans back, spreads her arms wide. The pistol is still pointing at her liver, give or take, but Alice won't shoot her now.

"The whole truth is bigger than me, Alice."

"Tell me the part I need to know," Alice says. "Tell me what you are asking me to do."

Prudence looks at her face. There's a lot of intelligence there. She'll only come on side if she believes in the rightness of it. Show, don't tell. The first rule of propaganda.

"If you trust me, I can show you why I need you. It will be horrible. Like nothing you've ever imagined. But you'll be safe. Well, safe enough. Well, as safe as I'll be."

Alice frowns even deeper, then points the pistol to the sky. Prudence thinks for a moment she's going to let off some kind of warning shot, blow a hole in the ugly drop ceiling, but Alice flips something down on the top of the pistol, shakes it to the side so gunpowder blows into the air, moves the hammer on top, then thrusts it into the holster at her belt.

"Good," says Prudence. "Now close down your portal so we don't get any more Georgian visitors, and I'll open one to the future. And then, I think, you'll understand what we must do."

They stand together as Prudence opens the shimmer. Only a fool would not hesitate at this threshold and she is not a fool. She tells herself she doesn't want this herself, as penance or as last hurrah.

"Ready?" Prudence asks. "Remember, just stand and watch. You'll be safe so long as you do what I tell you. And don't take that gun out, whatever you do."

Alice nods. "You lied, or were in error, about one thing at least."

"Hmm?"

"You said you're not my mother. But you don't know that, do you? You can't know it. It could happen in your future. It could happen in your past, if someone changes history."

She's right, technically. How old did Grace say Prudence is now? Thirty-eight? Something like that. Time travel is always there, waiting to call your bluff on your regrets. But not giving birth to a child is definitely not among Prudence's regrets. The change a teleosopher would have to make, for that to change in her makeup, would be a cataclysm.

And anyway, time travel will soon be impossible. One more day.

"Well? It's possible, isn't it? I could be your child?"

"I think the odds are low," Prudence says, in a voice she hopes is kind.

CHAPTER SEVENTEEN

On a Battlefield; and in a Ballroom

1916

ALICE LURCHES THROUGH THE aura and all her limbs shudder. Her heart is racing faster than it did when Grigson and the footmen were chasing her. She *believes* in her gut that her body has travelled across some vast divide—the sensation convinces her—but she reminds herself that the machine could be creating the sensation, that the whole thing could still be some sort of trick.

What it is, at the moment, is loud. Booms like cannon fire, rattling like many muskets at once, and the whinny of horses and shouts of men.

She and Major Zuniga are in a tiny, low-ceilinged room. On one side, there is a shallow, open window just at ground level; the room is mostly buried.

"I'm always a little surprised that this place is still here," yells Major Zuniga, but the noise is so great that

Alice has to stand even closer to hear what she's saying. "It's our training room, but it's as vulnerable to shelling as anything. First lesson of training: You're actually there. Always. There. Part of it."

Alice steps closer to the window, looks out. A bloody, muddied hand, the fingers dragging the earth, passes right by her and she steps back in shock, then looks out again. The man's face is contorted. He's being carried on another man's back. They're both in browns, greys, greens, and the man doing the carrying is wearing a metal hat. There's a line of men in those hats, like medieval crossbowman's helmets, with long guns at their side, wearily carrying their bloody colleagues as if there were not cannons booming, as if the ground were not spraying all around them.

It's hot and it stinks of wet ground and carrion. War. Much changed.

"We have to get out," she gasps. "The guns."

A flash of fire lights up the room like daylight. Someone screams, and runs past the window.

"We've been here many, many times," Prudence yells. "It never gets hit."

"But history changes! Doesn't it?"

"We won't stay long. All you need to know is that this is 1916, in France. Near the River Somme. Have you been there?"

Alice shakes her head. "I've never been out of England."

She wants to go to France. Mrs. Thackeray asked her to go with her, three years before, but she suspected Mrs. Thackeray would treat her like an object to display.

Alice's head is spinning and she wants to retch. She puts her hand out to the sweating wall to steady herself. Major Zuniga catches her arm.

"Look, now."

Alice steps gingerly to the window and peers out. There's a ridge of a kind, dotted with trees like gallows, painted in putrescence, and figures of men running up to the ridge, and falling. Gunfire so rapid it is one continuous drumbeat. Something whines, a sound Alice cannot place; it could be anywhere. It sounds as if it's overhead. She can feel the muscles in her jaw working, rebelling, feel the heat in her eyes.

"This was not in the history books, when I was born," Major Zuniga yells. "When I was born, there was no fighting on the Somme in 1916. In 1916, Austria and Hungary were ruled by a man named Rudolf. He was a liberal ruler, concerned with the welfare of his people, and so the Misguideds saw him as someone with potential."

She spits the word *potential*.

"What happened?"

Major Zuniga fiddles with something at her waist. The

quality of the light inside the portal changes to gold, and Alice thinks she catches a strain of music. She takes Prudence's offered hand and they step through

1888

and Alice gasps. The ceiling over her head is robin's egg blue where it is not whorled in gilt. Instead of guns, she hears violins, and people are dancing all around them. The women wear close-fitting jackets like redingotes.

The people smell of rosewater and wine. She is still ill from the stink of murder, from the lurch and then the other lurch. Bile rises and she holds her hand over her mouth.

"Careful," Major Zuniga murmurs. "If you vomit on someone's shoes, some gallant will think you're an easy mark."

Alice doesn't trust her voice. With her left hand still over her mouth, she holds up her right in a gesture that means every question.

"In Vienna, in the year 1888," says Major Zuniga. "That man there, with the enormous moustache and the medals and the thin face like a philosophy student? About thirty? That's our Rudolf. The Crown Prince. In the first draft of history, his father will abdicate in five years' time, leaving Rudolf to forge a better relationship with France, and Hungary and the Balkans, and to enact a number of liberal reforms."

"And is this the first draft of history that we're watching?"

"No. Not even close. See that girl he's dancing with?"

The girl is a doll, all curves and dimples, with black hair piled high and blue eyes. Her face is flushed with dancing.

"Her name is Mary Vetsera," Major Zuniga whispers. "In three months, he'll shoot her dead and then kill himself."

Alice turns to her, half-expecting her to be joking. But Major Zuniga looks angry. She's watching the couple dance, her body thrumming.

"Let's stop it, then!" Alice whispers.

"Don't tempt me, Alice Payne. It's my fault that girl dies. It was another girl, before, but I saved her, and doomed this one."

"But why must Rudolf kill anyone?"

"It started with the Misguideds trying to make things better, of course. Good intentions! They always have good intentions. They wanted Rudolf to be more sympathetic to women's rights, to avert the Suffrage Riots of 1917. The ones that happen in the history when the First World War does not."

"Suffrage? For whom?"

"For women."

Alice can hardly believe it. "It takes *a century and a half* for women to get the vote?"

Major Zuniga smiles, glances at her. "The point, Alice, is that it didn't work. The Misguideds and their tutors and good influences—it all certainly made Rudolf more liberal, and deepened the rift between Rudolf and his conservative father. Rudolf became cut off from his family and from any hope of power or any influence in government. His life began to seem futile, so he spent it on drink and sex. Instead of becoming a feminist, he contracted syphilis. Rudolf is actually quite a horrible person, even if he would have been a decent king."

Alice wants to ask about the vote for women in England, about slavery, about a cure for smallpox, about democracy. But Prudence is looking angry again, angry and sad, and the look on her face stops Alice's words in her throat.

"I spent ten years of my life trying to stop Rudolf's suicide from happening," Major Zuniga says. "Ten years in which I relived a single year, sometimes a single day, over and over. Ten years of Prince Morbid and his morphine habit becoming ever more ruinous to himself and those around him. I did not succeed, and eventually, I was reassigned. We gave up on 1889. We focused our war project on the agents we had in 1913."

"We're going there now, aren't we?"

In answer, Major Zuniga pulls her by the arm, back through the crowd, and reopens the portal.

CHAPTER EIGHTEEN

A Death Is Averted, by Means of Which Prudence Makes Her Case

1913

THEY EMERGE IN A FOREST, in the evening. Prudence has never been here before but she knows the coordinates. This mission exists because her own mission, the Rudolf Project, failed. A dove calls, and as if in answer, they hear the distant laughter of men, the bark of a dog.

Everything smells fresh and green. A lie; or a temporary truth.

"We're in your England now," says Prudence. "Well, not *your* England, of course. This is England in the third draft of history."

"Third?"

More like the seventy-eighth, but let's keep things simple. And let's speed things up.

"You have a choice, here, Alice. You can save a man's

life, in about, oh, four minutes and thirty-eight seconds. The year is 1913 and, thanks to my failure with Rudolf, Franz Ferdinand is the heir to Austria-Hungary. He's through those woods."

It is so beautiful, this English forest before the fall. You can walk through these trees as if they were the pillars of a cathedral. You can hunt your prey, so easily, although your prey will see you coming.

"He is here visiting friends," she continues, "and shooting pheasants. In three minutes, a man will stumble and his gun will go off."

"Well, why are we hesitating?" Alice asks, stepping forward.

Prudence grabs her arm. She holds out her arm and points toward the distant voices, and feels for a moment like Scrooge's third ghost. *Are these the shadows of the things that Will be, or the things that May be, only?*

"Wait. I am giving you a choice. If you let Franz Ferdinand die, that terrible war we saw will not happen. His nephew, Karl, takes the throne in 1916. He will pursue peace—at any cost. Half of Europe disintegrates on his watch. The wars are more scattered, but they last longer and are just as bloody. Women get the vote at least a decade later than they would if Franz Ferdinand had lived one more year."

"One more year?"

"That's option two. If you step forward now, and save his life, Archduke Franz Ferdinand will be assassinated in Sarajevo in 1914. It sets off a chain of geopolitical posturing that becomes the Great War, the First World War, the bloodiest conflict in the history of humanity. It sets the stage for an increasingly bloody century."

Alice makes a little incoherent sound of frustration. "You're telling me that no choice can be a good choice? Can nothing ever be *made* to get better?"

Yes, things do get better, sometimes. That's what kept Prudence going, all those years on the Rudolf mission. That's what kept her from pulling the trigger on Project Shipwreck, until now.

There have been great heroes, on both Farmer and Misguided sides. Great deeds done.

More often, when something gets better, it's the perverse result of the Misguideds and the Farmers trying to undo each other's work.

Smallpox eradication in the twentieth century is the classic result of serendipity, although both sides claim it as a victory now. The Farmers, suspicious of global institutions, tried to embarrass the World Health Organization by setting it up to fail. The Misguideds were trying to turn the Soviet Union into an upstanding member of the global community. And to everyone's surprise, the posturing actually wiped out humanity's greatest scourge, almost as a side effect.

Prudence could tell Alice about that, but Alice's hope would complicate things. She doesn't have ten years for Alice to go through the same process Prudence has, of learning the dangers of optimism. None of the successes make up for the failures. Humanity will be better off as it was before, without time travel.

She takes Alice's hand and looks into her eyes. Now's the time to make her believe it's all up to her, and make her believe she can't do it alone.

"There is a Farmer agent there with those men, ready to jog an elbow at just the right time and save Franz Ferdinand's life. The Farmers prefer that option to the Karl option. They've made their choices. You make yours. Do you want to run toward those men, now, and stop that Farmer from catching that man, and hope that the shot hits Franz Ferdinand? Hope that it doesn't spray into other people, and start other catastrophes?"

Alice frowns, looks out toward the voices. Any moment now. There isn't time, no time to think. Prudence very deliberately didn't give her any time to think. Alice will fail here, let a man die out of hesitation, and then she'll have just enough guilt to be useful.

The shots, oddly out of place, and people shouting.

Alice jumps, shudders.

"There it is," whispers Prudence. "The man lives."

"You didn't give me time," says Alice through gritted teeth. "I don't know why you've shown me all this, if we won't act."

"Because what I'm asking you to do is to act, Alice! To put an end to all this, and now that you know a little, you have to know everything or you won't do it. You have to understand why. We've made a horrible mess of it, Alice, and every time we try to repair the damage, it gets worse. There's only one way to stop it, and it will require all your highwayman courage, Alice."

Alice raises her eyebrows. "I hope our next stop includes whiskey, then."

Prudence laughs, for the first time in years beyond count, and the men beyond go quiet, as if they have heard something.

"We must leave," she says, and opens the shimmer.

2070

Prudence tells Alice to sit in Prudence's office chair, and she does, straight-backed as if she were in a drawing room with a cup of tea. She takes the little black box from Prudence, turns it over in her hands. Helmut designed its user interface with an eighteenth-century naïf in mind:

it has a mechanical button, in red-painted metal, with an aluminum wire cage over top.

"The cage is for safety," says Prudence. "You unlock it with this key, and then you depress the button. You will not notice anything, and no one in your world will notice anything. The only consequence to your life will be fifty thousand pounds, which you will find buried beside the milestone on Dray Road. It won't be there until July second."

"And if I change my mind?"

"Then time travel will continue to exist, which means I will go to July second and remove the reward. You'll go on with your life just as it is, but without the satisfaction of knowing you've put an end to an otherwise endless war that will just keep poisoning humanity's future and its past. And without the fifty thousand pounds. Then I will travel back a few days to find someone else to do the job for me."

It isn't quite that simple. The moment Prudence, Helmut and Rati press their own button and put Project Shipwreck into motion, sending more than two billion Misguided people five hundred years into their future, Prudence will be a fugitive. She'll have to find her new patsy in 1788 while outrunning General Almo and the rest of the TCC. But she has a plan B. And a plan C, and a plan D.

And she has no intention of telling Alice about Project Shipwreck. She doesn't need to know about that.

"I understand," says Alice. "I'm ready."

"Well, good, but I'm not. I have one last bit of time travel to take care of, so I need to do that before I send you back."

"I thought you said you would send me back with one hour to spare."

"Yes, but the moment I send you back to do it, it will have been done. Time travel will become impossible, the moment I change history by sending you back. I will no longer exist in 2070. I will exist in my own time, in the twenty-second century, and I will remember none of this."

She is fairly sure that is what will happen. If she exists at all. But she has been preparing for this martyrdom, for losing her memory of the life she has lived and per-haps even life itself, for a very long time. For three years, Helmut has been working on his EEG scanning and Rati has been shimmer-stealing to finance the purchase of the very large, very expensive twenty-second-century bacte-rial power cells that sit in the basement of this twenty-first-century suburban home.

They are ready.

"The moment we have done what we need to do, I will open a shimmer for you here in this room. You must step through it, without hesitation, as soon as it appears."

Alice nods, still looking at the device in her hands.

It is a sophisticated little thing, although it looks simple on the outside. It will emit a strong electromagnetic pulse at the same moment as the gravitational waves from the Dove Nebula hit the Earth. If that pulse were constant and predictable, time travellers could simply use that as their beacon. But it will not be. It will be a random, ever-changing signal. A beacon that changes, and should make it impossible for travellers to use a relativistic four-dimensional map.

Prudence sits in the chair opposite Alice, covers her hands in her own, looks into Alice's eyes. "Listen. I didn't go looking for you. But you came through, intelligent and courageous, a goddamn black woman making her own luck in eighteenth-century England, and I decided to see it as fate. A person starts to have a relationship with fate, after spending their life in time travel. You start to recognize it on the road. But fate is just a set of options you hadn't considered. The choice is yours. Alice, if you don't want to do this, tell me now and I will send you back."

Alice looks up with an expression that Prudence can't read, and says nothing for a long while. Then she smiles and takes a deep breath.

"I have a relationship with fate too. My father came home much changed from King George's long and pointless war in America. If I understand you correctly, this war of yours is making our wars even longer and bloodier. You can depend on me, Major Zuniga."

Prudence leans back, looks for a long moment at her face. "Then it's goodbye. And thank you. Remember, you'll have one hour before sunset. I'll return you to the place you left. The device has a timer that will tell you precisely when to press the button."

She looks long and hard at Alice, and then grabs a piece of paper and a pencil off her table and writes a brief letter, a last letter, just in case.

She thinks of Rudolf, writing his letters from Mayerling, loading his gun.

Prudence leaves Alice in her workroom and stands on the landing of the horrible staircase, the bright green carpet never clean. She won't miss this house; of course, if all goes well, she won't even remember it to miss.

She opens a shimmer one last time, delivers her letter, and steps back through.

Then Prudence goes down to the basement, where Helmut and Rati are eating ravioli cold out of cans and staring at the numbers on Helmut's screen.

"It's time," says Prudence. "My 1788 patsy showed up here, unexpectedly. I don't want to miss the chance. If I send her back now without the button, she's a tainted naïf who knows too much and could have all kinds of effects.

She's ready to go now, so we have to be too."

Helmut looks up at her, his face red, but he says, "I'm ready."

Rati says nothing, only nods. She looks at Helmut, and then lifts her chin and looks at Prudence.

"All right, then," Prudence breathes, and sits down on the ratty couch.

Rati's frantic journeys around the globe, shimmer by shimmer, have not only been for fund-raising by theft. She has also planted long-range EEG scanners in every major city. They won't capture every Misguided soul on the planet on June 29, 2070, but they will capture at least two billion.

Then those power cells will be put to work to lock on to each of those two billion people and transport them to the year 2555. Way downstream. Nobody knows what happens in 2555, because it's so volatile, so long after the beginning of the History War.

An entire generation of Misguideds, instead of being on Earth at the beginning of that war, will be absent. They can't affect anything, from so far downstream, not if time travel is effectively disabled. The world will be the Farmers' to shape for a generation, and that generation will matter. Its work cannot be undone.

Prudence Zuniga is not content to simply put an end to the unending war. She is going to win it first, for her side.

Project Shipwreck is a tactic her superiors long ago considered and discarded, because they couldn't fathom how they would prevent a counterattack. They did not, would not, consider disabling time travel. Only Prudence has the stones for that. Prudence and her two young radicals, whom she will never see or remember again.

"It has been an honour," she says. "On my mark, Helmut."

CHAPTER NINETEEN

In Which Jane Is Given a Commission

1788

WITH THE EXCEPTION OF the black mask, which is no longer on her face but tied to her belt, Alice is still dressed as a highwayman, from her cocked hat to her black boots, when she steps through the gateway into Jane's study and comes face to face with Captain Wray Auden.

His face goes from surprise to a sad smile, very quickly.

"I hoped I was wrong," he whispers.

Alice's heart seizes. She could step back through the gateway—damn, it's closed. Major Zuniga must have set it to open for a certain length of time.

But Jane can use the time-wheel, now, to get them away from here.

Major Zuniga's demonstration has convinced Alice of one thing: that the History War must end, that time travel can't be the domain of two armies bent on shaping the world to their will.

But beyond that, Alice does not know what to do. The thought of destroying time travel wrenches her gut. If she simply refuses to act, Major Zuniga will find someone else. And Major Zuniga can travel back in time to find someone else. Alice can't see a way to win.

So she has played for time, played the part of a convert, to get back to Jane. She needs Jane's help. She needs Jane's mind.

But Jane does not look inclined to even speak to her.

Jane is even holding the time-wheel in her hands, standing a little behind Auden. Her blue eyes are wide and she is staring at Alice as if she is nearly as surprised as Auden is. And of course, she must be. She did not know Alice had come to her study last night, had opened another gateway.

"Well," says Auden, having recovered himself, "now we have an answer to the mystery of why Miss Payne was not at Fleance Hall today, although how you manage to come and go like a stage magician is a mystery still. Perhaps when you explain that, we'll have an answer to how the Earl of Ludderworth was abducted. And at last, we have an answer to the mystery of the identity of the Holy Ghost."

Why doesn't Jane open a gateway?

"Are you going to take me to the lockup, Captain Auden?" She smiles at him, not looking at Jane, not giving him the slightest clew that Jane is her accomplice. She wills him to look at her, not to look around the room at the wooden arms and legs, to make the connexion between Jane's hobby and the Holy Ghost's silent partner. *Stay silent, Jane, for God's sake, if you're not going to get me out of here.*

"I must take you to the magistrate, and he'll decide where you should be kept. I will recommend that you be taken to another county. There will be an uproar, and unkind things in the newspapers."

"Captain Auden, I rob groups of armed men. Do you think I am afraid of unkind things in the newspapers?"

There's the sad smile again. "I do not think you can expect mercy, I'm sorry to say, from the newspapers or from the magistrate. Usually when we catch a highwayman, we offer him the chance to become a thief-taker and pay his debt to England that way, and save his neck. In your case, that will not be an option, of course."

"Oh, of course. It would be unthinkable that a woman could be a thief-taker." She lets him squirm for a moment, wondering if she is serious. Jane is stock-still. She might as well be an automaton herself.

And then Jane speaks. "If the magistrate will not show mercy, perhaps you can."

Auden turns to her. "I am bound by duty, Miss Hodgson, however horrible I may find it. I am sorry."

"Your duty, yes, is to bring her to the magistrate. But give her the small human kindness of a few minutes to get herself into decent clothing, and to say a private word to Colonel Payne."

Dear Jane. She is always thinking, that mind working away. Like the device in Alice's hand, so simple on the outside, so complex within. She has less than an hour, now, before she is meant to plant the device and secure the reward. The reward that Alice can never have, now. But Jane could.

"Miss Hodgson," says Auden, "I have never told you that I once knew a woman who looked exactly like you."

He's picked an odd time for small talk.

"I have almost asked you, many times, if you might have a twin sister," Auden continues. "But then I remember that this woman was, in 1780, older than you are now. Not to mention living in America."

"I have never been to America, I'm afraid. What was her name? Perhaps she was from a branch of the same family."

"I never knew her name. She was a supporter of the rebels. She came one night with a few other women to tend to the wounded. This was near Charleston. The colonel in charge was a . . . well, let us say he was a hard man. He ordered us to do something which would have haunted my dreams forever, if I had been forced to carry it out. To shoot the women in cold blood, as they tended to the dying."

"He changed his mind?" Jane asks.

Alice stands still, like a frightened rabbit, afraid that if she moves, everything will change and this truth will vanish. The truth that this woman was Jane. Jane was there, in America. And that means Jane goes on to use the device in her hands. It means Prudence fails.

Doesn't it?

"No," says Auden. "He did not change his mind. He did not show mercy. But one of the rebel women—the one who looked just like you, Miss Hodgson—she came very near to us, bravely, and said something to one of her companions about a nearby British camp being aflame. Grateful for an excuse not to carry out our orders, we turned and rode to help our compatriots. When we got there, the camp was perfectly well. That woman saved her own life and those of the women around her. And I have often reflected that she saved my soul as well, or at least saved whatever piece of it might survive that terrible war."

Alice only now realizes that she has been gripping the edge of Jane's worktable.

She wants to weep, and does not trust herself to

breathe. She may have no faith in humanity but by God, she has faith in Jane.

"I am perhaps too sentimental," Captain Auden says, too brightly, as if he too is trying not to betray some emotion, "but in memory of that woman, I will show what little mercy I can. I give her into your care for ten minutes, Miss Hodgson. Then she can say her farewells to her father, with me."

"Thank you," says Jane prettily. She does not know, does not suspect, that Captain Auden just told her the story of how he met her in America years ago, when she was older than she is now.

Or perhaps she does. Jane is always one step ahead, although she seems to stand still.

Auden steps toward Alice and speaks softly. "And because I was in the war with your father, I will do this for him, too."

"For Jane, then, and for my father. And not for me."

He looks down. "You know I have a great deal of regard for you. If our lives had gone differently—"

She puts her finger to her mouth, so that Jane will not have to hear any declarations. "I don't ask anything from you, Captain, other than these ten minutes. It will be a rush, to get this body into stays and stockings and gown in that time, but we'll manage it. For you."

He attempts a smile, and steps back. Jane is watching him, her lips thin. She is not watching Alice, as though she cannot bear to. Oh God, she's lost Jane. Alice is lost.

But Jane—Jane goes on.

Auden stands at the door, and then turns. "And Miss Hodgson, you may be wanted at the magistrate's as well. To explain how Miss Payne was able to secure one of your creations. Without your knowledge, I am sure."

Bless him.

"Captain Auden," Alice says loudly, "I have been pondering a question. And since it seems I shall never have the pleasure of asking it at a salon, would you give me your answer?"

He raises an eyebrow. "A question."

"Yes. A question. If you think of all the great mysteries of the past—the man in the iron mask, say, or the murder of the princes in the tower. If you had some way to find out the truth of these mysteries, would you? Or do you think it is best that some things remain hidden to all, now that all hope of justice has passed?"

"Hidden to all but God," he says, his eyes twinkling.

"Well, yes. Naturally."

That face changes again, and he goes serious. "No. I believe that we have a duty to learn what we can. Justice is not only about finding criminals and hanging them. Justice, I think, is another word for truth itself. Even a very old truth can still teach us something, help us make this world a less imperfect place."

She nods, and looks from him to Jane and back again. "Thank you, Captain Auden. You have settled my mind about something."

He is gone.

Jane and Alice stand looking at the door for a long moment, time slipping by.

"You did not even tell me you were using the device," Jane says at last, her voice small and thin.

"I thought— I did not consider—"

"You did not consider me because you never do," Jane says, whirling on her. Her cheeks are red, blotched around her freckles. "Alice, my love, you act alone, always. You have not given yourself over to me."

"Given myself over? I don't know what you mean. How can I? What ceremony can we perform, Jane? What token can I give you? Have *you* given yourself over to *me*?"

Jane stands very still, the time-wheel in her hand.

"Perhaps not," she answers. Alice can't breathe; her ribs are too tight around her heart.

Voices outside the door, loud and urgent. Damn Auden—did he change his mind about the ten minutes?

Jane looks at the time-wheel. "We must use it, now, and get away from here," she whispers.

"Captain Auden, have you seen Miss Payne?" It is Satterthwaite's voice, outside the door, and he is alarmed.

Jane and Alice look at each other, step closer to the door to listen.

"It is the colonel," says Satterthwaite. "He's gone wandering again. Mr. Brown—the groom, begging your pardon—saw him walking on the rocks by the river, and tried to persuade him to come away. There is moss there, and the rocks are wet. But the colonel would not be persuaded, or even make any sign he hears at all. Mr. Brown has gone straight back to watch in case he falls in, but he couldn't make him come home."

Jane whispers, "Your father will only listen to you when he is like this."

Alice nods. She glances to the window. There's a bit of stonework on the outside she can climb down.

"I'll go," she says.

"It's not safe. They'll find you. You can save him now, but what about the next time he goes wandering? When you are hanged and in the ground, who will help him home then?"

"I don't intend to hang. Not this year, anyway. I have it on good authority that there are some new fashions coming and I would hate to miss them."

"Alice, stop. Stop! Stop sending me away from you. Sometimes, I swear, you risk your life just to keep me at bay. For now, this once, let me be by your side. Your life is at stake. If we are to escape, we must do it now."

"Jane, we are going to escape. But I only have an hour."

"Ten minutes, you mean."

"An hour, before the device in your hands becomes useless. And there is something I must ask you."

Jane makes a little sigh of exasperation. "Another salon conversation topic? Really, Alice?"

"I have learned that the woman I saw, the woman who dropped the time-wheel, is going to put an end to time travel once and for all. She has been fighting a war for history, and the consequences are awful. Awful, Jane. I've seen some of them. And I don't know what to do about it."

"She is going to destroy the time devices? But I haven't had a chance—I haven't had time . . ."

"You want a chance to try," says Alice, coming closer to her. "You believe that it's worth trying. That even where humanity has failed, and failed, and failed, that you might succeed. That you can make things better."

Jane's face clouds. She nods. "I have to believe that, yes."

She takes Jane's hands and smiles, truly smiles. "Then you are going to save me, Jane. I know you will. I have been to the future, and I have learned one thing. Would you like to hear it?"

"Five minutes," calls Auden, from outside. "Hurry,

please. I need you to come with me, Miss Payne, as quickly as you can."

He wants her to come get Father too, bless him. She doesn't need to climb down the stonework. Jane will save her, or she will hang.

She takes Jane's hands.

"I know that if I were given the chance to live my life over a million times, I would love you in every one."

Jane shakes her head. A tear has welled in one of her eyes and rolls down her cheek. Alice has never seen her cry before, not even when the news came that her sister died in childbirth, when Jane had the letter in one hand and her half-knit baby's cap in the other.

She puts her hands on Jane's shoulders and kisses the tear away, tasting the salt on her tongue, and then puts her forehead to Jane's.

"I am not sending you away," Alice whispers. "I am asking you to save my life, and to change my life. I am giving myself over to you."

Jane kisses her, hard.

There is a pile of papers on Jane's desk, scribblings and drawings. Alice finds a bit of blank space and writes with Jane's pen, as much as she can manage in the few minutes they have. She folds the paper, hands it to Jane along with the beacon-kill device.

She is out of time, and still in her highwayman clothing. Captain Auden will have questions. Let him wonder.

"Father needs me now. If we meet again, Jane, everything will be different. Here is what you must do, before the sun sets."

CHAPTER TWENTY

In Which Some People Vanish

2070

THEY EACH STAND BEFORE the retina scanner and Helmut gives the command.

Prudence touches the button at her waist to open the shimmer for Alice.

And then, a few things happen within the space of ten seconds.

Helmut and Rati are no longer in the room. They belong in 2070, so the destruction of the time beacon should not make them disappear, unless they are random collateral damage from the changing of history. More likely, they have been caught up in Helmut's own algorithm and sent to 2555 with all the Misguideds.

Prudence expected that possibility. At the extreme, radical ends, the scanner can't tell the difference between the Misguided and a Farmer. Helmut and Rati were radicals. They knew it was a possibility too.

But Prudence has not disappeared. She is not living in blissful ignorance of time travel in the twenty-second century. She is still standing in the brown-and-beige basement in 2070, when a shimmer opens, and General Almo stands there, a stun weapon in his hand.

"Shit," Prudence says.

Alice didn't do it. Either she was always lying about her intentions, or she got cold feet.

It doesn't matter. Prudence knew this could happen. Time to go to plan B.

Prudence touches her belt to open a shimmer but nothing happens. She hits it, hard. Nothing.

"We've disabled your belt remotely," says Almo. "New technology. Isn't it useful? Anyway, I don't think you want to do that. We have Grace, down in 2555."

She has trouble swallowing, trouble getting her breath.

"Grace?"

"She went down with the other billions of Misguideds. Might have been a false positive, although she had tendencies. We have agents holding her there, to make sure you don't do anything else foolish. She is comfortable."

"What about her husband?"

Almo shakes his head. "Alexei Komorov is still here in 2070."

Prudence shakes her head. "But if you can still shimmer—if—but why didn't you come five minutes ago?"

Almo sighs. "It was deemed convenient, your attack on the Misguideds. Not my call. We have chosen not to undo it. It takes the Misguideds years to get involved in teleosophy. The Farmers have the upper hand now, even despite the Misguided counterattack that sends half of us downstream a century from now. It's all officially 'worth it.' But I'm afraid we can't officially condone what you did. And we certainly can't let you do what you were about to do."

To go back to 1788 herself, and kill the beacon.

Plan C. She is standing on a trapdoor, over an open shimmer to a village in Greece in 1779. It'll take them some effort to find her then and there, and in the meantime, she can work on killing the beacon. Again.

But Grace. They have Grace, in 2555. Separated from Alexei. In custody. Paying for her sister's sins.

"You are my fucking responsibility," says Almo, low, sad and soft as if he were reading a bedtime story. The tone he always used with disappointing recruits. "I made you. I let you run obsessed too long on the Rudolf Project. And now I have to fix my mistakes. Take you downstream and out of the mix, where you can't do any more damage."

Grace wanted to have a child. She wanted a normal life. She deserves a normal life. A life in a real house with real work to feed her real family. A life without a sister always looking at her funny, wondering whether this would be the moment where she winks out of existence.

She will have time—she can make time. Between 1779 and 1788, Prudence will have time to figure out a way to get to 2555 undetected and save Grace. But she is certainly not going to go there in cuffs, now.

She kicks the lever of the old reclining chair, to open the trapdoor, to slide into the past.

The lever slides down, the chair bounces into its upright position.

It is not connected to the trapdoor.

Perhaps there is no trapdoor. Not now.

"We have Helmut Kauffmann and Rati Kapoor too," says Almo. "Do you have a plan D? If you do, now would be the time to try it, because in five seconds, I stun you and drag you back through this shimmer."

CHAPTER TWENTY-ONE

Concerning a Rescue and
What Comes Before

1788

THE HIGHWAYMAN KNOWN AS the Holy Ghost lurks behind the ruined church wall. Lurking has a different quality to waiting, she reflects, having time for reflection.

Havoc raises his head and his nostrils flare. A horse comes down the road, from the top of Gibbet Hill: a horse he recognizes. Alice pulls him back a step, then she recognizes the horse and rider herself.

"Jane," she hisses. Could something be wrong at home? Is Father wandering again?

But Jane holds out her hand, the palm toward Alice. What in the Devil's name can she be thinking?

Ah! There it is. A carriage comes rattling around the corner, the horses' gait slowing as the slope rises toward

Gibbet Hill. That will be Lord Ludderworth, and Jane is about to sour the whole plan.

What a gaudy contraption the Earl of Ludderworth uses to get around the country, half-painted in gold as if he were Marie Antoinette, its four lamps lit although the sun is still bloodying the forest. Four horses, plumed. That dark bulk on the seat is the coachman and footman, both liveried like dancing monkeys, no doubt.

The carriage rattles to a stop and the coachman calls out, "Make way."

"I come from Fleance Hall with a message for Lord Ludderworth," Jane shouts.

The carriage window opens, and Lord Ludderworth's head appears there. "Miss Hodgson, is it?"

Jane walks her horse closer to the carriage door.

"My lord. Forgive this ill welcome. I have bad news. Miss Payne is stricken with smallpox. She is strong and stubborn and the doctors say she has a good chance to live, but we are to have no visitors."

"Miss Payne! Surely I can be of some help to her father in this time. I've had smallpox, you see, as a child."

So has Alice. What can Jane be doing? It isn't her way to pull a private joke; that's more Alice's province.

Lord Ludderworth doesn't ask whether his coachman or footman have had smallpox, nor his manservant, who must be in the other seat in the carriage.

"It's very kind of you, my lord," says Jane. "Very Christian indeed. Even if Miss Payne lives, she is very likely to be disfigured."

"Ah, I see. Well then. What a bloody shame. I say, Brown, Greenleaf, have you both had smallpox?"

"I haven't, my lord," says the coachman.

"Oh dear. Well, that does it. We'll have to turn around. Please send my compliments, Miss Hodgson, and I will send . . . what shall I send? Oranges? Yes, oranges. Before the week is out. Grigson!"

A man comes riding around the corner, just behind the carriage. Ah. His manservant was riding behind—to chase a highwayman, should one appear? Perhaps Jane got wind of that, and is saving Alice from it. As though Alice could not have handled it perfectly well.

She snorts in frustration as the carriage disappears back the way it came. Havoc stamps.

Jane rides to her, stops alongside.

"You are going to have to trust me a little, now," says Jane. "Can you give yourself over to me, just for a few minutes? Some things have happened. I will tell you what I can, but we must go now. Up the hill."

"Is it Father? Wandering again?"

"He is in good hands. We are going somewhere else. We are going to meet a woman named Prudence Zuniga, and we are going to convince her not to make a terrible mistake. It might take a few tries. She is very set upon it, I'm told."

She turns her horse and rides up the hill and Alice, speechless, follows.

Jane pauses at the old milestone. She pulls a brass device out of her saddlebag, some instrument with wheels on wheels.

"I hope I can remember the correct setting—you've been mucking about with this."

"I haven't. I never play with your toys, unless you ask me to."

"Shush. Keep still and let me do my work."

Alice looks up and down the road. It is getting dark, under the trees. It is unlikely anyone will pass this way before morning, now, but all the same they should dismantle the automaton. All that work she had setting it up, all for naught.

Something is fluttering on the side of the milestone. A moth? She dismounts and ties Havoc to a tree. It takes a bit of work to winkle the paper out from the crack without tearing it.

"What is it?" Jane asks, looking up from her device.

"A note, or something. A lovers' assignation? How marvellous!"

She peers at it in the dying light. "Very odd penmanship. Very odd message, come to that. Wait, it's meant for me! I think."

Jane is on foot now too, and comes to her side. "What does it say?"

Alice reads:

PLAN D

If you have been clever enough to return to this time, Alice, it means you have changed your mind, and you are going to try to change mine.

I left the time-wheel you found in your possession so that if you changed your mind, this would be how you changed it.

If you get this note, it means that I have not been able to return to kill the beacon myself—because if I do that, I will be there an hour before the beacon-kill to make sure you can't shimmer back to this time.

If you get this note, it means that something goes wrong. I would like you to bring it to me, so that I know that too. It means that I have chosen to leave this here for you to find. Bring it to me, please.

And have patience. I can be a little stubborn.

PZ

She turns to Jane. "I can't make head or tails of it. What

have you been hiding from me, Jane? What is going on?"

"PZ stands for Prudence Zuniga. The woman we have to find, now, and persuade."

"Persuade to do what?"

Jane shakes her head. "To change her mind. Beyond that, I don't know much. I do know we'll do it together, this time. Everything is going to be different. Kiss me, and then take my hand, because I don't know what happens next."

The Most Recent Draft of History

1756: Alice Payne is born in Kingston, Jamaica

1759: Alice and her father come to England; he buys Fleance Hall

1778: Alice's father goes to America to fight (Alice is 22)

1783: Alice's father returns, wounded

1784: Wray Auden buys New House

1788: The Earl of Ludderworth goes through a time portal

1889: Crown Prince Rudolf dies in the Mayerling Incident

1913: Franz Ferdinand narrowly escapes death while hunting in England

1914: Franz Ferdinand is assassinated and the First World War begins

1916: The Battle of the Somme

2038: Discovery of time travel

2040: Prudence and Grace Zuniga arrive in Toronto as child refugees from the future

2070: Prudence, Helmut and Rati set up Project Shipwreck

2071: Teleosophy begins

2091: The Berlin Convention on Organ Manufacture

2092: The History War begins

2131: Grace is born

2132: Prudence is born

2135: Invention of wireless remote EEG scanning

2139: The Anarchy begins

2140: Prudence and Grace are sent back in time by their parents

2145: Teleosophic Core Command

Acknowledgments

I thank, first, the many real women whose lives or work inspired elements of this book.

To my family, all my gratitude for their constancy, and especially to Brent and Xavier, who are forever patiently waiting for me to "just finish this thought."

My thanks to Jennie Goloboy and everyone at the Donald Maass Literary Agency, to my editor, Lee Harris, and the whole wonderful team at Tor.com.

I thank David Thomas Moore for his encouragement and support.

To the Zuniga family, who offered me food, shelter, friendship and lessons in life and Creole many years ago, my thanks.

Thanks to Aidan Doyle, Megan Chaudhuri and Em Dupre for reading an early draft in whole or in part and providing their feedback and encouragement. I am grateful for my writing community, and I thank in particular the members of Codex for help with the research and brainstorming for this book.

Any errors or oversights are mine alone.

About the Author

KATE HEARTFIELD is a former newspaper editor and columnist in Ottawa, Canada. Her novel *Armed in Her Fashion* (ChiZine Publications) was published in 2018, as was her interactive novel *The Road to Canterbury* (Choice of Games). Her short fiction has appeared in several magazines and anthologies, including *Strange Horizons* and *Lackington's*. Her website is heartfieldfiction.com and she tweets at @kateheartfield.

TOR·COM

Science fiction. Fantasy. The universe.

And related subjects.

*

More than just a publisher's website, *Tor.com* is a venue for **original fiction, comics,** and **discussion** of the entire field of SF and fantasy, in all media and from all sources. Visit our site today—and join the conversation yourself.